Five Days in Autumn

Published by White Elk Press, an imprint of Aspen Mountain Publishing, Sugar Hill, Georgia.

http://www.whiteelkpress.com

Printed in the United States of America

ISBN 0-9777237-2-0
ISBN-13 978-0-9777237-2-0

Library of Congress Control Number: 2007932026

First Edition

Edited by Julie Wallace and Carolyn Smith
Cover design by eLEMENT-d

Acknowledgements

I want to thank Julie Wallace and Carolyn Smith for their tremendous contribution to the development of this project. Without your keen eyes and editing abilities, the story line would have been buried beneath my penchant for wordiness and random thoughts. I owe you a huge debt of gratitude. I want to thank all the folks who gave me feedback when I asked and who contributed to the many wonderful memories I have of my youth. I also want to thank White Elk Press, especially Tom Stanton, for believing in this project and making it a reality. Many others, too numerous to mention, were unknowing, but invaluable, contributors to my character development process. You hold a very special place in my heart, and I hope I represented the beauty of east Tennessee culture in a way that makes you proud.

For Annie

TABLE OF CONTENTS

MONDAY..........1

TUESDAY.........25

WEDNESDAY....71

THURSDAY......117

FRIDAY............156

MONDAY

As I held her, a single tear traveled slowly down her cheek, mirroring the depth of emotion we had just shared on this rainy, autumn night in the mountains of east Tennessee. I thought back to all that had happened in the last five days, and how quickly life can change. There have been times in my life when things have happened to me and, most of the time, I didn't know why, but this time I understood everything perfectly. At any other point in my life, I would have told you that things like this didn't matter to me. That just about everything else was more important and more deserving of my time. I see now how wrong I was…and how close I came to missing my chance to figure that out. But let me take you back to the beginning. I need to explain a few things.

I am one of the millions who is his job and whose job is him. Intertwined, interconnected, and running 24/7 from meeting to meeting, airport to airport, and country to country on wireless connections and high levels of caffeine. We're like sharks—if we stop moving, we die—or at least lose our edge to those nipping so closely at our Gucci-soled heels. It's a race to the end, and it is all I think about. A good day for me is getting to the office early, attending meetings, making powerful business connections at lunch, and closing out a few more things after everyone else goes home. Achieving more, taking on more. Need an answer to a question on the weekend? No problem, give me a call on my cell. Want to send me a note to review on Christmas Day? Feel free, my Blackberry is always on. If nothing else, send me an email and I'll pick it up on my wireless laptop wherever I am.

And I'm not alone, I don't believe. People in my age group have no idea about certain basic tenets of life. Our pace has become so quick and hectic that our measure of a good day comes largely when we've checked off most of our to-do list, ensuring our continued livelihood for at least one more day.

You may think I'm the product of an urban upbringing; a child of two career-centric parents who shipped me off to boarding school fall, winter, and spring and lined up a plethora of fascinating camps to occupy me over the summer. But actually, I am the product of a mountain upbringing; a little hamlet in the hills of east Tennessee. There wasn't much there then, and there isn't much there now. My parents were simple, down home folk who were content with what they had and never felt much of a need to venture beyond our county line. My father was a night foreman at a local mill and my mother, aside from a brief foray into secretarial work at our church, was a homemaker who basically took care of my father and me. It was a relatively simple, predictable existence.

Yet, I never felt as if I belonged there. I was captive in a place that time and culture had forgotten. From a very young age, I told myself I would leave and never come back to that place unless forced to by the law or death, the latter being the preferred reason as it implied a lack of consciousness. So when I passed the magic age of 18, I enrolled at a major university miles away from home and left.

A few years later, I graduated with honors with a degree

in Finance. Though ready to continue my education at a higher level, I decided I wanted to see the world before committing forever to a life of suits and secretaries. So, I joined the Navy to see the world. She was my salvation, and upon her vessels I toured the four corners of the globe, and beyond. Those travels filled my mind with new ideas, thoughts, and all of the possibilities that the world held. I found the enlightenment I needed and cherished every minute of it. Upon discharge, I enrolled in a master's degree program focusing on international business. My career took me through various levels of increasing responsibility until I landed where I am today—Sr. Vice President of Global Development and Acquisitions for a large, multinational corporation based in Atlanta. I am where I want to be, and I plan to stay here…no matter what the cost.

I've been very successful in my career up to this point because I get results, and the world of business rewards results. What's implied in that, however, is that you will get the results in a way that doesn't hurt or kill anyone (or even make them cry). If you do harm someone, you aren't living up the values your employer has told God and everybody they live up to (even if they don't). And, to put it in the vernacular of our younger years, 'you get into trouble.' Well, I got into trouble.

It was Monday October 15 and I had raced down to my office overlooking the Atlanta skyline to make an early conference call with our Frankfurt office. I was preparing to dial-in when the shadow of my boss, Mike, our chief operating officer, filled the door. It was not unlike him to drop in to chat, but it was rather unexpected to see him so early in the morning.

"Carter, we need to talk." I felt myself sink back in the chair, fighting the adrenaline suddenly coursing through my body. That phrase, as generic as any other, can define moments of your life when, whether you realize it or not, life changes.

He closed the door, sat down in the wingback chair across from me, and smiled weakly hoping to break the tense air he had created. When failing, he continued.

"Carter, I admire good work ethic and you definitely have that. If I want something done right, I bring it to you and I know it gets accomplished. I don't have to worry about the quality or the accuracy."

"Thanks, Mike. It means a lot to hear you say that. I—"

He held up his hand to cut me off and continued.

"But I also look at how results are gained. To be blunt, I am very concerned about how hard you drive the people who work for you...and especially yourself."

That was completely unexpected. I fumbled for the right words. "I've put everything I've had into this job ever since I arrived and if I've screwed up, well..." I paused and waited.

Everyone has their critics, but I admit I top the list as my own worst. I was a perfectionist in every regard with my work, and equally demanding of others. Success had been my driver, this uncontrollable urge to produce faultless results without considering my own well-being. Even the slightest hint of a mistake on my part caused me significant anxiety.

Mike sighed. "I wish it were that. THAT I could have a brief conversation with you about, shake a finger in your face, and tell you not to do it again. Then I could buy you a beer and that would be it."

Being more curious than apprehensive now, I looked at him with an expression that I knew must look like an inquisitive dog.

"There are some things in life I feel strongly about, and the well-being of my employees is one of them. When I don't think things are as they should be, well...I feel like I have to intervene."

I stared at him as he continued.

"And, even though they do not report directly to me, I have a responsibility to those who work for you. They are raising concerns about the expectations you have of them. They don't feel your expectations are humanly possible to achieve. I hear reports of long hours, consistent weekend work, and performance feedback that is more critical than balanced. As a result, they are completely demoralized, totally overwhelmed, and don't feel they are doing anything right. That's not a good state for a department as critical as yours to be in."

He paused, waiting for a response from me, but received none. Seemingly uncomfortable, he cleared his throat and leaned forward in the chair before he continued.

"I'm thinking you need to take some time off, to distance yourself from this place. From where I sit, I see someone completely wrapped up in his job and that's not healthy. It's not healthy for you because if your job ever went away, and I am NOT suggesting that is happening, what would you be left with? Granted, it's a personal lifestyle choice for you, and I respect that, but as long as you report to me, I feel I have an obligation to look out for the whole person."

What would normally incite an energized response was met with only silence. I felt a numbness wash over my body.

"I...I don't know what to say," I whispered, worrying the pen in my hand with increasing pressure, "I've never had this happen to me before..."

"Had what happen?"

"Called out for a performance issue..."

"But you don't HAVE a performance issue," Mike explained, sounding exasperated. "You perform exceptionally well. I'm just concerned you work TOO hard and you need a break...and I think your people need a break, too. We're between projects right now and there's nothing earth-shattering that can't wait. Take the week off. Go some-where. Do something. Do anything. Personally, I think you'll find yourself recharged and even more productive after some time off. And who knows? Maybe you'll discover something new or rediscover something you'd forgotten. But don't think about this place. In fact, I'll only call you if I need you. If you don't hear from me, everything is fine. Normally I would ask you for your thoughts on the matter, but since this isn't negotiable, I won't insult you by even asking." He looked me dead in the eye to reinforce the point.

I looked at him for a moment, trying to keep a small tide of panic at bay.

"Mike, you've always been straight with me and I don't want you to stop now. I have to know…does this mean my job is at risk?" Mike's directive and message were so unexpected, and unlike anything I had ever received, that my first thought was that he was going to fire me.

Mike leaned back in his chair and looked toward the window.

"Carter, I'll be honest. Right now, no, your job is not at risk." He turned his gaze back to me. "But if things don't change a little around here, it very well could be. I can't deny that I need you to take the well-being of your employ-ees, and yourself, into account more than you have. I fault myself for not being more on top of this than I have been. I fear that you've taken my complacency as an OK from me that we can keep working this way."

He was right. I had.

"But that's not the case. I expect the very best of people when they are here, but only within reason. If everyone gets burned out and quits, I have nothing. And you have nothing. No one wins in the long-term scenario, and that is simply unacceptable. So, the sooner you understand what I'm talking about, the brighter our future will be." Mike flashed the smile I'd seen too many times before indicating he was done with a topic and was not open to negotiation.

Unable to keep it at bay any longer, a riptide of panic washed through me as my intuition began reading between the lines. He was pleased with my results, but now he didn't like the way I managed my group...even though I had been doing everything the same way for years. The reason seemed a little too convenient, too sudden, and he didn't deny that it could compromise my job. But I'd been around Mike long enough to know which battles to fight and which to let go, and this wasn't the time to pick up my sword.

"OK, I get the message...out until next Monday." I didn't know what else to say, and I certainly had no idea what I was going to do for a week.

He stood up to leave, but paused first.

"Thank you, Carter. It will be good. Trust me." The cynic in me becomes riled and reactive when instructed by another to trust them. In this case, I had no choice, but that didn't mean I did.

"One last question—do I need to take your Blackberry?"

Ow. That hurt. For those of you unfamiliar with such a wonderful creation, it is a handheld device that gives you wireless access to your email, calendar, the internet, and any other information that you can send or receive. It's wonderful. In fact, many people have taken to calling it a 'Crackberry' because of its addictive power. And I was addicted.

"Considering it's also my cell phone, I would really prefer you didn't ask me for that. Otherwise, you won't have any way to reach me," I fibbed, frightened by the prospect of losing my connection to the only world I knew. I did have another cell phone, but only used it for personal calls so my reasoning for keeping the Blackberry WAS honest, in a creative sort of way.

Mike thought for a moment.

"OK, but I don't want to see email from you...or even hear about email from you, until Monday. In fact, come see me first thing when you're back next week. I'll be curious as to how you enjoyed the week."

He closed the door and left me in silence. Joining the conference call didn't make much sense at this point as most of the participants likely gave up on me and moved on to other things. My computer was pinging with new email every fifteen seconds or so, but from what I now understood, I shouldn't touch it. What do I do now? Take a trip? To where? Call someone to go do something? Call who to do what? I literally had no clue what to do next and, for me, that's extremely rare.

Then I noticed a familiar email address in my inbox: Lee37604@aol.com—my mother's email address. Though my mother's everyday life was relatively unsophisticated, she had embraced, and eventually figured out, the online world. Granted, she thinks 'spam' is a canned meat product and 'Googling' is something you do to someone you think is cute, but she can find her way around the internet well enough to be effective...and dangerous. Her email address was a product of her last name and her zip code—easy to remember and relay. God forbid either one ever changed.

From: Lee37604@aol.com
Sent: Monday, October 15, 2006 7:36 AM
To: Lee, Carter (Atlanta)
Subject: Monday

i am going to need your help this week taking care of daddy....the doctor wants tom to have a procedure...........I think he'll be laid up for a few days...........your aunt had to go out of town all of a sudden and can't help so please come and sit with daddy.........let me know when you are com-

ing........just moving along up here otherwise........
everybody is enjoying cooler weather.........will get
my church picnic over next tuesday night and will
be glad........ luv, mom

Today's message was not as serious as the email advising me that my grandmother had died (yes, death notice via email), but it imparted an unexpected urgency. "Daddy" in this case is my 87 year old grandfather and Tom is my father. That's about all I can interpret and, as with many of her emails, I become frustrated because of what it does and doesn't say. What procedure is my father having? Why is he going to be laid up? Why do I need to come up? Who cares about the weather? And why do you use so many periods?!? The last question is the most perplexing of all, yet right now, it is the least of my worries.

It's not often my mother makes a direct request like that. Normally she is very respectful of my schedule, and obligations, but this seemed different. I don't know the particulars of the situation, but obviously I have to go and, apparently, I now have the time to go. I picked up my personal cell phone, dialed my mother's number and waited for the phone to pick up.

"Hello?" answered a quiet voice, with a twinge of a Tennessee accent.

"Hi, Mom. It's me. I got your email and I've rearranged my schedule to come home and help you out." No need to tell her why I could rearrange my schedule and come home on such short notice.

"Are you sure, sweetheart? I just hate so much being a bother like this, but I just don't know what else to do." This phrase uttered by my mother, one I've heard over the years, means that while I feel somewhat bad about inconveniencing you, I don't feel bad enough to turn down your help. But I'll be apologizing to you for at least the next day or so until I feel better about it all.

"Yes, Mom. It's fine. It actually worked out well with my schedule. I'll leave shortly and be on my cell in the car if you need me. You do have the number, right?"

She paused before answering.

"Could you give it to me again? Just so I know I have it by the phone?"

Slightly exasperated, I gave her my number again for what seemed like the 1,000th time. It's not that I mind giving it to her; I just wonder whether she could find the number if she really needed to reach me someday.

"I'll see you in a few hours, Mom. I love you. Bye."

So there I was, on an autumn morning in the bustling city of Atlanta, Georgia, a high-ranking executive who closes deals worth millions and dines with execs from all over the world, sitting at my desk pondering how my world has turned so upside down. The events of the past hour shattered the familiar tension of my morning, much like an autumn leaf breaks the surface of a quiet country pond. It's one thing to have a bad day; it's quite another to be 42 years old and be told by your boss to disappear for a week and by your mother you have to come home. What a week this was shaping up to be.

There is a country song I recall from my younger days that says, "Sometimes you're the windshield, sometimes you're the bug." Today I was definitely the bug, smacked into a gob of anger, surprise, and fear. I'm not really sure why I am angry, but since it feels appropriate at the moment, I'll go with it. It certainly doesn't make sense to be happy. The feelings of surprise and fear, however, were completely expected and not ones I am used to.

Surprise because I had no idea that both a forced sabbatical and an obligation to care for an elderly man was coming at all; fear because for the first time I did not have my security blanket of work to cling to. I was a junkie cut-off from his supply, and the withdrawal was already starting. I had my Blackberry, but instead of alleviating the anxiety I felt, it only exacerbated it as I could read email but had been told NOT to respond. Inhumane torture of the worst kind. And whispering in the back of my mind was a small voice asking, 'Was Mike telling you the truth or is this just his prelude to pushing you out of your job…your job that is your life?'

My anxiety worsened the minute I left my office. I realized I had to find something other than work to do during the next week while I sat with my grandfather. While most people could choose items to fill their time from a mental list of family activities, personal hobbies, or books they wanted to read, I could not. If a task or event did not relate to work, it did not occupy my world. This week now represented a dark vacuum, a portion of my life I would be consciously wasting and would never recover. Or so it seemed to me. It was like I had been asked to plan a dinner, but I had no recipes to use and I couldn't even cook. I was completely unprepared and helpless.

I winced at the thought of what the week would hold for me with my grandfather. Sitting. Doing nothing. Watching an old man continue to wind down his years. Sharing the decay of passing time. Purposeless? I felt so. But sitting with the sick and dying is a peculiarity my mother feels very strongly about. She is reluctant to let anyone be alone, no matter if it's a meal, a birth, or a sickness, so I didn't feel as if I had much choice in the matter.

Normally one would pick up the phone and call friends or family to commiserate and vent with, but I did not have that luxury. My circle of friends had slowly contracted over the years due to my lack of time to maintain the relationships, and the last of my non-work acquaintances had dropped off several years ago. I was left with family who, though well-intentioned, could not understand the emphasis I placed on my career and work. Thus, we had very little to discuss beyond the benign topics of weather and local updates, and very little common ground on which to build any relationship beyond the cursory.

My grandfather's life was completely opposite from mine. At this stage of his life, he was confined to a hospice in the same little town that was his birthplace. Aside from a few years in college, that same little town was his home for his entire life. I guess he figured you may as well close the circle of life in the same place you started, and Sweet Branch, Tennessee, had been a good place for him to be. He had conducted business, worshipped, played, and raised family and crops all within the comfortable confines of one county. It was a simple enough existence, and one that had served him well. So well, in fact, that he refused to leave the county to die, even though it would have been tremendously less burdensome on my mother and aunt to move him to a facility closer to where they lived. But his daughters could not deny his dying request to stay close to home.

For several months, my mother had spent the weekday hours sitting with my grandfather in his small private room at the Sweet Branch Hospice Center, simply being there and attending to his relatively few needs. Since her home and his facility were a decent distance apart, she spent nights at the family farmhouse then drove home to Johnson City whenever my aunt took over. For the next week, it would be me who would occupy that house and sit in that chair beside my grandfather. Not really knowing what to do or even why I was there, aside from a sense of unbearable obligation, I knew I would never live down the guilt from my mother if I refused. I resigned myself to my fate.

I started the car and headed for home to pack a bag for the trip. My home is not a house per se, but an upper floor condominium in a new development overlooking a revitalized section of Dunwoody. If you're young in Atlanta, you typically gravitate to the sights and sounds of Buckhead where you can play and cavort with those of your own age and hormone level. As a single male approaching his mid 40s, however, I was more interested in the convenience and potential appreciation of a Dunwoody property. Besides, I didn't spend much time there, so my real estate investment should at least earn me some money in my absence.

Without the worries of a purposeless pet to board, I was changed and packed within an hour of getting home. I inventoried my cell phone and Blackberry chargers, laptop, computer case and assorted peripherals, and sealed up the bag. I fought the urge to turn on my home computer and check my email as I needed to stay focused. Lingering over email that I was instructed not to answer would only delay my departure, and I wanted today's drive over quickly. I was not in the mood to sit in a car today, and Atlanta's rush hours can be three-hour convergences of a million people wanting to go a million directions all at the same time. Heading from the northern suburbs to downtown around mid-morning can easily turn into a two-hour event. Luckily, however, my trek would take me northward against the flow of traffic and into the rural areas of Georgia made famous by such classics as the *The Dukes of Hazard* and *Deliverance*. With any luck, I could be at my parents' house in five hours.

I loaded up the trunk, paused long enough to collect my thoughts about locking up the condo, and climbed into the leather driver's seat of my BMW 750i. Normally, I look forward to a drive like this to stretch the engine and get the full benefit of the power plant nestled inside her sleek hood. But today, I dreaded the journey like the plague. Redundant stretches of open road would force me to replay the same events of the morning over and over in my mind. The secure feeling of connectedness I usually gained from my Blackberry and wireless devices would simply mock me, reminding me of my exile whenever the topography of the area permitted them to work. Even radio, the seemingly ancient workhorse of automotive communications, would be challenged to provide any distractions as my journey would take me in and out of multiple listening areas. For now, I would need to be my own company.

Heading north on I-985, I watched the miles tick by as billboards and businesses gave way to open pastures and splashes of natural color more vibrant than the grays of city concrete and metal. I rolled down the window and listened to the loud drone of the air passing over this open space that now disrupted the aerodynamics of the car.

As a young boy, we only had 4/60 air conditioning in our one sedan; 4/60 meaning four windows at 60 miles an hour was the only way to cool the car in the heat of summer. I would ride in the backseat, staring out the window on the long trip from our house in Tennessee to visit various relatives along the East Coast. I would relax and disappear into the silence of the wind, but today the drone mirrored the blankness I felt. I wanted to become as transparent as the wind and simply drift along like an anchorless boat in churning surf, to be seen by no one.

The trip felt as if it would never end, each mile seemingly longer than the previous one as I crossed the state line into Tennessee. I finally pulled into my parents' driveway around 4:00 p.m., turned off the car and instead of getting out, just waited for a moment. I felt so out of place here that it took awhile to re-acclimate to the familiar, yet foreign, surroundings. Though I know I have a history here, I no longer felt a connection to this world...the world of my youth...my parents' world. I don't picture myself as 'better' or 'above' those here, but I did feel different, and sometimes being different can be uncomfortable.

And that's where I found myself on this autumn day—facing the transition back to my past while still hurting from the pain of my present. Maybe in some ways it would be a blessing to be back in this simpler environment for awhile. At least, that's what I could hope. With a sigh, I got out of the car, grabbed my luggage from the trunk, and headed up to the front door.

"Hi, Carter," my mother greeted as she opened the faded, lightly warped screen door. "Did you have a good drive up? I was afraid you'd hit some rain between here and Asheville."

"Yes, Mom, it was fine," I replied as I kissed her on the cheek and wondered why rain would be an issue. "It wasn't very crowded."

I hesitantly put my bags down and looked around for a clue as to where my father was.

As if reading my mind, she said, "He's resting at the moment. The doctor does not want him to be very active before the surgery. That hasn't been a problem, though, as he feels just terrible."

"What exactly is going on? It wasn't clear in your email and you didn't say when we talked." I asked trying not to sound agitated about being told of a potentially serious situation with my father via email, without a semblance of what was going on.

"Gallbladder. Doctor thinks it's his gallbladder and I think he's probably right. He's had such pain in his chest, and his stomach doesn't seem to do well with most of what I make him." I had to chuckle as a steady diet of my mother's menu of southern 'comfort' food could give a goat digestive problems. "They're going to take it out tomorrow, prayin' nothin' else is wrong. At his age, though, it will take him awhile get back to full strength again. That's why I needed you to go to Sweet Branch to be with your grand-daddy." She paused, then looked up at me with a sad look. "I don't think he's got much longer…but I have to be here," she lamented as her voice trailed off.

My mother and my grandfather had always been very close. Though she never expressed it, it seemed that the transition from her role as her father's child to his caregiver was difficult. She now had to be his rock when for years he had been her compass, her anchor...her constant. I struggled in a way to understand that closeness, mainly because I had never experienced anything like it.

"What time do I need to be there tomorrow?" I was thinking mid-morning would be sufficient. It was a 70 mile drive, but unlike in Atlanta traffic, I could easily make that trip in under an hour.

"Tomorrow? Oh, I was hoping you could go down there tonight..."

"Tonight?" My voice was reaching for octaves it had not visited since my late teen years.

"Well...yes...it would be nice if you could be there...close by...just in case. I usually try to be at the hospice center around 9:00 a.m...." She looked at me as if she was going to plead, but I saved her from that humiliation.

"OK, Mom...tonight it is."

"And you'll be there at 9:00 tomorrow?"

I sighed under my breath.

"Of course, Mom. Whatever you need me to do."

Relief washed across her face as at least one obligation she had placed upon herself was met. For some reason, having someone near my grandfather, despite their limited usefulness at this stage of his life, was important to her. Who was I to deny this simple desire?

Over the course of the next two hours, I visited with my father, ate a sandwich of country ham and block cheddar cheese, an apple picked recently in nearby Unicoi County, and my father's favorite cole slaw. I suspected the slaw was leftover from my mother's efforts to find something that he could eat...or would eat. I only hoped she was focused enough to monitor its expiration date; otherwise for me, it would be quite a night.

I reloaded my bags into the car, kissed my mother good-bye, and took off for Sweet Branch. My brief time at my parents' house had made me forget the reality of my day, but returning to the contents and confines of my car brought the stresses back, albeit they were slightly diminished.

As I pulled out, I looked at my Blackberry for a moment before giving in to the urge to check my inbox. "NO SERVICE" glared at me from the upper right corner of the color screen. No connection with the outside world only increased the feeling of isolation growing within me. Though only 70 miles, the drive to Sweet Branch was going to feel much longer.

Sweet Branch is a small burg just before the sprawling community of Morristown, Tennessee. My family migrated to this area back in the early 1800s after arriving from the eastern coast of Scotland around what is known as the Kingdom of Fife. It was a long running joke that we were descended from royalty, only because of the name of the area from whence we came. Nothing else about our ancestors would support a claim to royalty or nobility, but instead a simple life of farming and public service to God, community, and the generations that would come behind them.

My grandfather seemed to be cut from that same mold. He was a gentleman farmer with a penchant for entrepreneurial projects. A family man who supplemented the living made from farming with income derived from various businesses and profitable ideas. I speak from a distance about him because I never really knew him, for whatever reason.

Throughout life, you meet people who you are very close with from the very moment you meet them. There are others with whom you eventually form relationships that rival familial ones, even though they may take awhile to grow. And then there are others who, no matter how many times you enter their space and engage their minds, never move beyond a handshake and a warm smile. They never open-up beyond the obvious, and leave you with very little on which to base any type of relationship. That was us. Most little boys relate back to fond memories of their grandfathers around fishing, woodworking, or a host of other hands-on hobbies. But not me.

And that is what made this obligation so incredibly difficult for me. Aside from everything else going on with me at the moment, I was now obligated to spend an isolated week with a dying man whom I did not really know, and who really didn't know me. I could stop at any long-term care home along any given highway, randomly pick a name from a list, and go sit by this person's bed. It would be about the same level of association and connection as what I had with my grandfather. And it probably would be just as convenient.

What bothered me the most was that I really wanted to know my grandfather. I remember when growing up how all the adults would talk about him in such glowing terms and speak about how much they valued his friendship. When you hear people talk of someone in that way, you want to be close to that person, to be one of their favorites...one of their chosen. But as much as I wanted it, it never happened, and I felt like I had missed out on not only a grandfather, but the influence of a very special man. But we don't always get what we want.

I pulled off the four-lane and turned onto the two-lane that meandered along the river back to my family's farm. The farther from the four-lane road I drove, the fewer houses, trailers, and other indications of domestic life presented themselves. Even now, I knew just what to expect around each bend and over each gentle hill, although the years had left their mark. The trees appeared to be taller, and the bushes wider, than when I had spied them through the back window of my parents' car. It made me wonder how I would look if I had remained here, instead of venturing out beyond the confines of my mountain home.

Though the path to the farm was as familiar as yesterday, what I saw when I arrived at the farm was not. Years of neglect had turned the once green pastures into an array of brush and brambles dotted with the ambitious presence of red cedars. It was obvious that neither cow nor tractor had entered these fields in many years. The house, once crisp in brilliant white, now bore an almost grey pallor capped with a peeling, faded, green tin roof. Along the front porch, a gutter had fallen from the weight of wet leaves, brush, and other debris that had accumulated over the years, transforming a formerly quaint scene into a poignant statement of the transitional nature of life. I was caught off-guard by the wince of regret I felt at seeing the farm reduced to this state, but even more alarming was the reality that this is where I would reside for the next five days.

I stopped the car and again checked my Blackberry for signs of life. Nothing. I was slowly resigning myself to complete isolation and the inability to reach anyone, at any time, for the next several days. Coupled with the likely lack of any type of television reception (cable was just too much of a stretch), I was going to be my own entertainment for the better part of a week. Mike wasn't just punishing me; he had condemned me to the worst personal hell possible.

As I got out of the car, I was met with a light breeze touched with the heavy scent of boxwoods. Boxwoods reminded me of cemeteries, as every graveside service I ever recall attending seemed to be by a large grove of the aged evergreen. Yet they seemed rather appropriate for this setting and the memories they stirred within me. Hopefully this was not an omen of some type, I thought.

I gazed around the countryside and paused for a moment to let the view sink in. The farm DID sit on one of the more beautiful tracts of land in eastern Tennessee, at least in my opinion. Positioned on a knoll, the house afforded an almost 360 degree view of the area. To the south and east were the Appalachian Mountains, tall and dark in the dying afternoon light. To the north, less commanding hills rolled softly from side to side up the horizon while a long tier of red maples lined a small ridge to the west, gloriously illuminated as the setting sun danced behind them. There were no neighbors in sight, which is not uncommon for rural farms. The aloneness was very present and very real.

With my gear collected, I stepped onto the worn gravel path that lead to a wooden front porch in dire need of repainting. A rail attempted to support me, but its ability to support anything—let alone me—appeared tenuous at best. The floorboards creaked loudly as I walked across to the heavy wood front door, and I wondered if I would even make it to the door or end up falling through to the ground below. I pulled out the large metal key my mother had given me and fumbled for the lock opening in the dying light.

Click.

The door protested my attempt to disrupt its solemn slumber, but reluctantly gave way to the space it protected. As if opening the tomb of some long-dead pharaoh, I was met with a gust of stale air, tinged with mothballs, which caused me to draw back in disgust. Though the sun still cast dim light on the outside of the old farmhouse, the inside was dark as pitch. I put down my bags and tried to peer into the blackness, but it was futile. Without knowing the layout of the room, I had no clue where to go. It made me wish for a moment that I was a smoker, so I could have a lighter or a match to illuminate the darkness. Then I remembered I still had my cell phone latched onto my belt which, though questionable as a communication device at this point, did have a bright screen that could give me a hint about where to go. I opened the phone and welcomed the glow that helped see my way to the wall switch.

Despite my hope, the light did nothing to lift the gloom I had perceived in the darkness. It was as if time had stopped, sealing the room in a period long gone, complete with the furnishings of two generations past. Stark white walls carried oval pictures of people I did not recognize, but could only assume shared my genes. Mad-looking people, at that. A sofa and loveseat draped in crocheted blankets lined one wall while a piano, table, and a rather large bookcase filled most of the remaining spaces around the room. A rug of some sort filled the area between the furnishings and there was an old desk tucked into a corner and covered with stacks of books and old legal pads.

I realized that there was likely no food, coffee, or anything else in the house I would need for the next week...or at least nothing I would want. It had not crossed my mind to stop on the way in and pick up supplies, and to top it all off, I was getting hungry. This was going to be an interesting adventure, and not one I could handle on an empty stomach. The grocery store I remembered from years ago was miles away, but if I didn't buy something to eat tonight, I would regret it in the morning. I dropped my bags onto the floor and turned to leave.

"See you in a bit," I mumbled over my shoulder to no one in particular. Luckily, no one responded.

After half an hour of traveling back roads and four-lanes, I found the grocery store and loaded up on canned spaghetti, rolls, coffee, cereal, milk, beer, and a bag of chips. My view is that shopping when one is hungry suspends any obligations to proper diet and nutrition. And thank goodness Starbucks began selling their coffee in grocery stores a few years ago, otherwise I would really be in trouble. As I was leaving the grocery store, still hungry and growing more tired by the minute, I saw a small diner advertising a fried catfish dinner with all the fixin's for $4.99. Sounded like a good deal to me.

After a dinner that acclimated my body to a cholesterol level it had not experienced in years, I headed back to the farmhouse in the autumn darkness. Many years had passed since I had driven through the countryside in the dark. Accustomed to city streets brilliantly illuminated by street-lights, road signs and billboards, the darkness of the winding back roads presented a challenge. Maybe country folk do get conditioned to drive slowly, I reasoned. Driving too fast around here at night could be deadly.

Before I even finished the thought, a pair of bright eyes suddenly appeared in the middle of the road in front of me. As I slammed on the brakes, the possum turned towards the sound of my screeching tires and immediately rolled onto his side. I smacked the steering wheel in frustration, muttered a few expletives under my breath, and waited to see what he would do. It would have been incredibly unfair of me to take him out just after sparing his life, as much as I wanted to at that particular moment. But Mr. Possum just laid there, feigning death; a defensive strategy configured into him millions of years of ago that seems reasonably successful, considering their numbers. I didn't have the patience for him to reason through his stress, though. Not tonight. I was tired, and he was the only thing between me, the farmhouse, and a good night's sleep. Since I had no real intention of killing him, I slowly began to move around him, driving into the other lane to bypass him completely. It was at that moment I saw the lights of another car coming over the hill directly at me.

Instinct took over and my foot slammed the gas, bringing all cylinders of the 750i to life in a sudden roar. With both hands on the wheel and groceries flying across the backseat, I was barely over the yellow line before some type of large vehicle came within inches of sharing my paint job. I slammed on my brakes for the second time in the span of a minute just to make the crazy experience stop. Despite the adrenaline rush, all I could think of was, did I hit that possum after all?

In my side view mirror, the taillights of the other vehicle slid to a stop, the driver's side door flew open and a figure moved briskly towards my car. Illuminated by my taillights, it assumed the persona of a demon in flight determined to take me to Hell.

"Are you CRAZY?" I heard someone shout through my closed window. Suddenly a dark shadow of the face that owned the voice appeared right next to me, only a thin sheet of safety glass protecting me from this raging woman.

"What in the world were you thinking driving in the other lane? Are you insane?!?!?! You could have KILLED me!" The verbal torrent raged on from this potentially deranged individual. OK, time to wind this up, I thought.

"Sorry, lady!" I hollered through the still closed glass as I hit the accelerator. This time, I was careful to stay in my own lane, but to get as far away from this raging loon as I could. Luckily, between the winding roads and perfect handling of the BMW, it was doubtful she could turn around and catch up with me…at least, that's what I hoped.

In several minutes I was in the drive of my grandfather's house and out of the car quickly, so the cabin light would not give away my location in case she followed me. I stopped and listened for the sound of an approaching car, but heard none. In fact, I heard nothing at all. Complete silence; save the rustle of the wind through the boxwoods and the mourning cry of a far away train. Silence was not something I was accustomed to, and its presence was a bit unnerving. Sound to me meant life was around me. But in this place, silence and the enveloping darkness beckoned all kinds of thoughts and images of childhood fears. Whether or not it was real or a product of my now stimulated imagination, I perceived movement of some type out of the corner of my eye. Some type of animal, dark and low to the ground, appeared to move around the corner of the house and down into the back field. It made no sound, but the faint moonlight cast its silhouette against the side of the house. Then it was gone.

Lovely, I thought to myself as I quickly collected the scattered groceries from the backseat and made a beeline for the front door. Between nearly dying for the sake of a possum, a confrontation with a crazy lady, and a brush with...well... something, this was not going in a good direction.

Though my earlier impression of the house did not make me look forward to returning, I was relived to be inside and away from the oddities of the evening. The long road trip, and the stress of my job and family situation, had left me with just enough energy to change my clothes, find the bathroom, and fix a makeshift bed on the sofa before calling it a night. Any expectation of exploring the house, and finding a real bed, would have to wait until tomorrow. All I wanted was sleep, and if there were ghosts in the house, I thought to myself as I drifted off, I don't care as long as they're quiet.

TUESDAY

When I was young and had a bad day, I would pretend that all the unpleasant things that happened were swallowed up by the darkness of the night. As I slept, all the hurt, anger, and tears I had experienced that day would be caught up in the darkness and slowly disappear as the night turned into yesterday. The next morning, things were either better than I remembered, or not as bad as I recalled. A new day gave me a new perspective.

Years later, I found that belief no longer held true. The house and my mood were just as dreary and depressing as they were the night before. Usually my day began at 5:00 a.m. with a trip to the gym, but at 7:30 a.m. I was still laying on an old couch in the middle of Green Acres in my sweats and a ratty t-shirt. Not that I had to be anywhere anytime soon. I wasn't on a schedule of any particular importance, so why not lay on the couch a little while longer, I reasoned. As my eyes adjusted to the light, I slowly scanned my surroundings, reconfirming the room and its contents. Nothing new, nothing amiss, nothing of any particular interest. The eclectic mix of heavy wooden furniture appropriately accented the age and style of the house. Obviously, my family had believed it was worth buying quality because quality would last. These pieces may outlive me, I thought. Rather charming, in a fatalistic sort of way.

It had been years since I had been in this house, and it had been awhile since I had been to Tennessee for any particular length of time. The most recent visit I could recall was for my 20 year high school reunion several years earlier. The only recollection I had of that trip was sitting around reminiscing with my classmates, and how idealistic the memories and emotions were from that time in my life. My youthful surplus of dreams, and the belief that nothing was impossible, had been replaced by realities requiring only logic and reason. I didn't dream any longer. Time didn't allow it, and my adult world didn't appreciate it. Thoughts and dreams only lingered with me momentarily before my work required me to push them aside and keep them out of my conscious mind indefinitely.

But as I recalled that time in my life, I started to wonder if over the years I became consumed by work to fill a void left by the loss of those youthful hopes and dreams. Dreams give you the feeling of purpose, and hope fuels the belief that the world is yours to be conquered. We charge forward with a feeling of invincibility simply because we're too naïve to believe anything is impossible. That drive remains with us into adulthood, but often times it morphs into something quite different...quite sullen. It's one thing to persevere out of an inherent need to chase a dream; it's quite another to do so as a means to escape the spirit of emptiness you feel staring at you from behind. Far enough away to be out of sight, but close enough for you to know it's there. That's why I despised solitude mixed with inactivity at this stage in my life. Being alone with my thoughts made the absence of any life purpose beyond my job that much more real, and that was a dark horror I fought to keep buried inside of me.

What I feared most was coming face-to-face with the fact that I had lived 42 years and had nothing lasting to show for it. My success had provided material means beyond what even I had expected, but that was all. In situations like yesterday, I had no real network to fall back on to support me emotionally, nothing to cushion my fall or limit the threshold of my pain and fears. The way I lived was all I knew and had served me well...but the flaws and weaknesses became all too apparent when things didn't go so well. So there I lay, alone in a house three times as old as me, and I had no idea what to do with myself to keep these feelings buried. For the next week I would be face-to-face with the emptiness of my life, and I had no place to hide.

Heading to the kitchen, thankful for my late night trek to the store for caffeine and other supplies, I looked around for anything closely resembling a coffee pot. Eventually I found an old percolator, which I wasn't sure how to use, and measured four tablespoons of coffee for every six ounces of water, a recipe I learned from a blonde barista. She taught me that making doubly strong coffee, then cutting it with 1/3 whole milk and sweetener of your choice, could get you a pretty decent coffee drink in a pinch. At least something good had come out of that relationship.

As I waited for the percolator to do its thing, I wandered back and looked around the living room in the growing light. In my haste to leave Atlanta, I had not brought anything with me to occupy my time while I sat with my grandfather. No iPod, no magazines, and certainly no work materials, so I needed to find something to occupy my mind. I walked over to the desk I noticed the night before, stacked high with books and legal pads. Picking up an older looking book from the top of a stack, I flipped through it. It appeared to be a handwritten journal of some sort. The others in the stack had the same worn leather cover around yellow-edged pages. Not seeing any other books or magazines in the room, I pulled several of them from the same stack, putting them in my backpack for later. Better than nothing, I reasoned.

The percolator finally finished its task and I took my coffee concoction and headed to the back porch to wake up with the morning. The air was the typical eastern Tennessee October crisp; not too cold, but indicative that the warmest part of the year had passed and a different season was taking its place. The sun was above the horizon, but a little fog still lingered in the lower parts of the field behind the house, glowing in the morning sunlight. The one constant I noticed between the night and the day was the silence; still present and still unwelcome as it made me be alone with my thoughts. I had a feeling this would be the first of several difficult days I would spend with my grandfather, silently waiting for death to arrive. There was no other way to look at it.

Though my mind took for granted he was dying, I found myself still longing to know more about his life. The idealism you place upon your grandparents when you are a young child never really leaves when you enter adulthood. They are nearly supernatural in their wisdom and caring and, though they lay dying before your very eyes, a small part of you still wants to believe that they will find a way to become who they were again. The way they were again. The grandparents you knew. The irony of the situation was that my grandfather might spend his last days with the grand-child who knew him the least. Somehow that just didn't seem fair.

My thoughts were still sorting emotion from reason when I felt I was being watched. To my left, silhouetted by the morning light, I saw the dark shape of some type of dog. I had not been around a dog in years, so my first reaction was one of caution. I waited for a moment to see how it would react to my presence. Every animal is different, and since I had no idea where this one had come from, I wasn't going to take any chances. When it didn't move, I slowly turned my head in its direction and in the calmest voice I could manage said:

"Hi, there."

Immediately, the large dark head cocked to the side and a tail, which had been invisible just seconds before, began wagging back and forth in the light.

"Would you like to come over and say hi to me?" I slid to the end of the chair to see if the dog would come. It slowly stood up and trotted over to where I had the back of my hand out for it to catch my scent. While I became familiar to the dog, I checked quickly to see how I should be addressing it.

"Well, hi there girl. Aren't you a sweet one?" She was a deep brown retriever of some type, not too large, but by no means small. The eyes that had been watching me in silence were almost golden in their color and took me in with an honest acceptance I never see in people. Her coat was rich and lush, the only blemish being a white or gray patch of hair on her right ear. It stood out against her dark coat like snow on a freshly-turned garden.

"You are obviously well-loved, my dear," I told her as I stroked her head. I was at least a foot from her head, but even from there I could smell the fragrance of what must be a very high-end pet shampoo. Flowery, but not repulsively sweet.

"Who do you belong to? I bet that was you running around in the dark last night, wasn't it?" The size and shape would have been right, but why a dog that seemed to be rather pampered would have been running around in the dark was illogical. Besides, where did she live? The closest house was at least two miles back up the road.

"Are you hungry? I don't have any food, but I could probably get some on the way home tonight."

Tonight. Today. What time was it? Crap. I looked at my watch and realized it was already 8:30. I had been 'instructed' that I should be at the nursing home by 9:00 a.m., so I would need to hurry and get ready.

"Sorry, girl. I lost track of time. Gotta run," I said as I rubbed her head quickly and rose from the chair. The soft golden eyes just looked at me as I gathered up my coffee cup and hurried inside. As the rusty screen door shut behind me, she stood up and quietly disappeared.

"Good morning, Sadie. Anything new with anyone last night?"

"Good morning, Jessica. No, nothing new. Mr. Hankins is still with us, but for how much longer, I'm not sure. Give me a few minutes and I'll give you a report."

'Anything new' was Jessica's way of asking whether anyone had died during the night. Jessica Cooper was a registered nurse at the hospice center in Sweet Branch and had been for the past several years. Earlier in her life, she was living the fast-paced, high dollar lifestyle of a private equity consultant in Washington, D.C. Her natural financial acumen and subtle drive were in high demand by those looking for lucrative businesses in which to park their loose millions. Jessica lived for her equity work and had built a stellar and well-deserved reputation for what she did.

But when her mother became terminally ill with cancer, Jessica had moved to the area to care for her. Jessica practically lived at the hospice center for months, from morning until night, providing whatever care she could and doing whatever the nurses showed her how to do for the dying. It was during that time, struggling with the new role of caregiver to the one who had been her caregiver for so much of her life, that she realized the limitations of her skills in regards to serving others. She felt helpless more often than helpful and felt there was more she should be doing.

One cold February evening as she sat with her mother, she noticed a subtle motion out of the corner of her eye. She looked and saw her mother's frail fingers reaching for her through the slats of the bedrail. Jessica rose and went to the bedside, her eyes meeting her mother's tearing eyes.

"It's time," her mother mouthed and reached again for Jessica's hand. Jessica wrapped both hands around her mother's and waited for whatever was coming next. She had dreaded this moment, and despite all the times she had coached herself to be strong, she felt completely unprepared. Her mother looked into the very reaches of Jessica's heart and whispered, "Thank you for taking care of me...I love you so very much..." Jessica squeezed her mother's hand and felt her tears begin to flow, her heart's acknowledgement of this final goodbye. She leaned down to kiss her mother's forehead and place her spirit against hers just one more time upon this Earth. They stayed that way for several minutes, Jessica watching the rise and fall of her mother's chest become slower and slower. With a gentle squeeze of her daughter's hand, Carol Cooper closed her eyes and as a light snow began falling outside, quietly passed away.

For weeks after her mother's death, Jessica stayed in Sweet Branch clearing out personal effects and the lifetime of memories her mother had accumulated. Though her employer had promised her job would be there whenever she was ready to return to Washington, she could not shake the feeling that that part of her life was over. She needed more now. Years of her life had been dedicated to making money for herself and others; now she needed to feel as if she was making a difference...giving instead of getting.

With her inheritance, her savings, and skills she had learned in her Washington life, she would have the financial resources to make a change in her life. Besides, she had learned that life was made up of much more than just money. She enrolled in a two-year nursing program at a local university and, upon graduation, went to work at the very place where she had helped her mother pass from this life. It seemed to be right, and she had never regretted the decision.

As she waited for Sadie to give her an update on the ward of ten patients in her care for the day, Jessica noticed a man in the greeting area who looked somewhat lost. Tall, clean-cut, straddling the line between a man of youth and a man of age, his eyes looked around for what he was supposed to do first, and what he should even say. Noticing the receptionist was busy with another family, Jessica walked over to the man.

"Can I help you?" Not only do you look lost, you don't look like the typical local, she thought.

"Yes, I'm here to sit with Mr. Jack Bailey for a few days. His daughter might have told you I was coming."

Jack Bailey was one of her charges, but she was not aware of a new caregiver. His two daughters usually took turns in the seat beside his bed, waiting for the inevitable with him.

"No, I'm sorry, I was not aware of an aide coming to be with Mr. Bailey. I'm his nurse. Are you a nursing assistant or just a paid caregiver?"

The man looked surprised.

"Uh...actually, I'm neither. I'm his...grandson. Carter Lee."

Jessica could not hide her reaction. The man's demeanor had not indicated a relationship with Mr. Bailey other than just a duty or a responsibility. Most family members caring for loved ones are proud to indicate their relationship. He seemed quite the opposite.

"Oh. OK, I see, Mr. Lee. Which daughter is your mother? Gertrude or Claire?" This was a trick question as the daughters were really named Mary and Helen. She had gotten to know both of them quite well over the last few months as they had spent so much time at the center. It was at least worth a shot to see if he was lying.

"Gertrude or Claire? For Jack Bailey? I think you're confusing him with someone else. My mother is Mary and my aunt is Helen." The man looked even more uncomfortable by now.

"Oh, sorry, yes that's right. Forgive me, I handle a lot of patients each day and all the families start running together. I can take you to him in just a few minutes. We're finishing up reports and it shouldn't be long."

She left him in the waiting area with last fall's issue of Golf Digest and a community television permanently locked on the Game Show Network. It was not unreasonable he was related to Jack Bailey, she reasoned. Both had the same straight noses and defined chins, but the tell-tale giveaway was the marble-blue eyes that had to be a genetic mark of the Bailey clan. In any other situation she might have found Carter Lee attractive, but when it came to her patients, she was as protective as a mother hen. Everyone should spend their last days surrounded by love; it was a privilege to give that gift to someone, she thought. A person who did not understand that, but basically viewed it as a burden to bear, was not a person she particularly cared for. While he had not said anything to indicate that was how he truly felt, something didn't feel right about Mr. Carter Lee, and her instincts were usually accurate. She would give him the benefit of the doubt, but he had a long way to go to change her first impression of him.

My interaction with the nurse did not make me feel any better. In fact, it made me feel even more apprehensive about what I was about to do. It wasn't so much the fact of being here and fulfilling the obligation of the dutiful grandson, but the fact that I was uncomfortable about my role. Being one of the last people that he would be with in his final days, yet knowing him the least, didn't seem fair to either one of us.

I sat in the waiting area watching reruns of $100,000 Pyramid and flipping through a year-old golf magazine. Finally, the nurse came back.

"I'll go back with you now," she said.

We walked down a long hallway that smelled of antiseptic and cleaning products, passing rooms occupied by people who were living out their last days. They had come to this place to pass on to another life, just like my grandfather. For some it was a blessing, for they were suffering and the closure of death would bring final and permanent relief from their pain. For others, however, it was sad because once they became residents of this place it meant there were no more chances, no more dreams or opportunities. Their life was coming to a close. All they could do was wait.

We reached the end of the long hallway and stopped at room 152. Through the door I saw a bed with a blanket draped over a figure. I hesitated for a moment, then moved into the room. There in the bed was a figure that barely resembled the vibrant, full-of-life grandfather of my youth. Crisp features had been replaced by the sagged, wrinkled skin of an old man. A dying man. Hair once neat and trimmed lay askew on his head in dire need of a haircut. His skin, unshaven and pale, hung from his face as if in an eternal pout. While the grandfather of my memory practically glowed with life, this person lay quietly in the bed with no indication of consciousness.

"He won't know you're here," said the nurse, as if reading my mind. "His cancer is so far advanced that all we can do is keep him pain-free, which requires a lot of sedation. I don't know how much longer it will be. At this stage, it could be any day. Or it could be longer than we expect. People can fool you. It's a wait and see situation."

"Is there anything I should or shouldn't do while I'm here?" I asked the question because basically I didn't know.

"No, not really. We actually take care of the patients at this point. The families come to be with the patients, but it's more for the family's benefit to be here than it is for any assistance on our end. You have your reasons for being here, I'm sure." She paused for a moment to gauge my reaction.

I sensed a bit of agitation with me on her part, but had no idea why. It struck me as odd, as we had only met five minutes ago, yet there was something that told me she did not hold me in too high of regard.

"You don't have to check in with me when you come and go. As long as we know who you are and why you're here, you're free to go in and out of the center as you need to."

"Thanks, I appreciate your help. If I need anything, I'll let you know. Otherwise, I'll just be here."

After she left, I took my backpack and moved over to the seat next to my grandfather. It seemed to be as good a place as any and, considering there was no other seat in the room, it was my only option. I looked around, taking in the green institutional walls, whose color was chosen to provide peace and comfort to those who inhabited the room, the cold linoleum floor, and the patient monitoring equipment. There was a TV mounted on the wall, but I did not feel comfortable turning it on for fear of disturbing him. Instead, I just stared at my grandfather's face. He looked so different from what I recalled, yet so familiar. I guess that's what old age does to you, I thought. He looked so pale and so motionless I couldn't help but wonder, are you still here?

Finally, I turned my attention to the contents of my backpack and the journals I had brought from the house. I had some hesitancy about taking them at all, much less reading them, as I assumed they were personal journals or diaries. These could be private thoughts and dreams. Who was I to invade them? But since I was desperate for reading materials, and there was no one around to tell me otherwise, the journals were my only option for distraction.

The journals smelled of old paper accented with mothballs and musty leather. Glancing down the first page, the writing was instantly familiar. This was my grandfather's journal. As I looked through the first one, I saw that my grandfather had dated the first and last pages of this journal, and I could only hope he had done the same with all of them. By sheer chance, I had picked up one of the earlier volumes as the date was April 5, 1939, when my grandfather must have been in his early 20s. My grandfather's handwriting filled the book from cover to cover, an unthinkable exercise in this age of email and electronic transcription.

Over the course of the afternoon, I read each page of each journal I had taken, absorbing the words and trying to understand the reasoning that would motivate a man to document his life like this. These were the opening annals of the history of a life. If future journals matched this pattern, there would be a journal for just about every year of his adult life. Unbelievable.

Though years separated us, many of the issues and questions he had were not unlike the ones I had had at the very same stage of life. It's funny how time brings us advanced tools of technology, but some of the basic, most core things about human existence never really change. Happiness, fear, sadness, frustration; they are all present in every eon of time, no matter whose life it is.

As I closed the last journal I had brought, I felt a range of emotions; amazement at the detail he provided to awe at some of the insight he voiced through his writings. His words demonstrated the richest and most private of feelings. He probably never intended them to be exhibited to me, but I was the recipient nonetheless. Though I had been there for over eight hours straight and he had not moved or spoken, I felt strangely connected to my grandfather and energized by the day I had been able to spend with him through his journals.

I was contemplating the words I had just read when the nurse who brought me to the room this morning came in to check my grandfather's vital signs for the third time that day. As she worked, I watched her fingers move nimbly up and down his arm, taking his pulse and checking his respiration. While she worked, I studied her features. Growing up, I was used to a certain look to the people in the area. Not ugly, not beautiful, just very solid and basic in their appearance. She, however, had a much different appearance. Long auburn hair, pulled back in a ponytail, deep green eyes, sharp, pointed features nearly doll-like in their proportion. Maybe it's true that men are only drawn to women who don't want anything to do with them, I thought.

"You have to be careful driving around here," the nurse said. "People around here aren't the best of drivers and they tend to fly around the corners of the back roads."

Her comment caught me off guard. "Sorry?"

"When you leave tonight. Just a warning. Be careful." Her demeanor did not indicate any care, compassion, or concern about my personal well-being. Maybe it was simply a public service announcement she was preprogrammed to deliver, I thought.

"I don't have much room to talk," I sheepishly admitted. "I was driving home last night and swerved to avoid a possum and about took out a car coming in the other lane. I don't think the driver was very pleased about that."

His comment surprised her. That was YOU, she said to herself. She was on the way to drop off dinner for a friend who had been ill the past few days. She had just crested the hill past Springer's farm when she saw two headlights moving quickly toward her in her lane. Jessica didn't have to swerve as the other car moved quickly into the other lane, but it still scared the bejesus out of her. And she had let the other driver know it...in this case, Carter Lee. It did not appear he got a good look at her, she thought, otherwise he would have said something. Funny. A grown man sacrificing life and limb to save the life of an old possum. Maybe Carter Lee wasn't as coldhearted as she thought.

"That sounds familiar," she smiled. "Had that experience myself once or twice." The formality she had exhibited up until now fell from her like a curling leaf from a tree in autumn. "I'm Jessica, by the way. Jessica Cooper."

"Carter Lee. Pleased to meet you." Their hands touched politely, and then lingered for just a moment before Jessica pulled away. Carter cleared his throat.

"I appreciate your guidance earlier today, by the way. I have never done anything like this before and my life is usually so regimented that I haven't had to learn anything new for awhile."

"Really? What do you do?"

"I work for a company in Atlanta. I'm like an accountant, I guess." That's a stupid way to put it, Carter thought. You just demoted yourself.

Jessica smirked. "Sounds complicated. Do you like living there?"

"I do. Most of the time. It's not as big a city as it seems. In fact, I think Atlanta is easier to get around in than Chicago, Houston, or LA."

OK, now you're sounding pretentious. Stop it. Change

the subject, Carter told himself.

"Have you ever been there?" he asked.

"Yes, a couple of times. Some friends and I like to shop in Buckhead and I have to admit it's nice to have choices in restaurants, shows, and museums all in the same town. Plus, there is a Starbucks on just about every corner." Jessica smiled, a warm smile that complemented her eyes and gave way to a subtle dimple in the corner of her cheek.

"You really have been there if you know all that." Carter was a little flustered at this point, partly by the attraction of her openness and warmth and partly by his embarrassment that she probably knew more fun things to do in Atlanta than he did. "My job keeps me so busy that I rarely get a chance to do anything for fun." He paused, gazing at her. "You may have to show me around your favorite places some time, if you're ever down that way again."

Jessica felt the burn of his blue eyes and had to fight the corners of her mouth from curling up in a silly, girlish grin. They stood there for a minute, neither knowing quite what to say next.

"You probably find the smallness of this area stifling."

He paused for a minute. "Well, to be honest, it has its own kind of charm for me. I've found it grows on you after awhile."

"It's definitely grown on me. I moved here about five years ago. It's not a bad place to be."

"Do you think you and your husband will stay here awhile?" He was fishing and knew it. It was just a cheap ploy to find out information.

"Oh, I'm not married. I have my work and a couple of acres not far from here. I have enough to keep me busy. Does your wife like living in Atlanta?"

"I'm not married, either. I have enough to keep me busy."

Another uncomfortable pause invaded the space threatening to ruin what had been, up until now, a very enjoyable conversation.

Carter felt strangely nervous so he reached down to pick up his backpack, just to have something in his hands. Jessica noticed this and took it as a sign he was ready to leave. She quickly noted Jack's vitals on his chart, returned it to the foot of his bed, and pointed towards the door.

"Heading out?" she asked.

Carter had not planned on leaving at that particular moment. Though seeing as she apparently either needed to leave or was thinking he needed to leave, he figured it was as good a time as any.

"Yes, I guess so. It's close to dinner time and I need to figure out what I'm eating tonight," he offered, knowing full well the limited menu that awaited him at the farmhouse. They moved toward the door, Jessica leading the way. A faint whiff of her perfume caught Carter's attention, distracting him for a moment before he realized she had turned to face him in the hallway.

"Well...have a good night," said Carter. "It was nice meeting you. See you tomorrow."

"Yes, you, too. See you tomorrow."

Jessica turned and began walking toward the rear of the building, realizing only after committing to the route that the nurse's station was on the opposite side.

No sense embarrassing myself at this point, she thought. I'll just wait a bit until he's left the building. He probably thinks this is where stupid rednecks are born and bred, anyway. No need adding to that perception.

Carter Lee hurried through the front door and out to his car, hopefully fast enough to get on the road before she could see his car. For whatever reason, he suddenly felt very self-conscious about his job and his car. It was unlikely she even made $70,000 a year, much less would understand why someone would pay that for a car.

He sighed. "She probably thinks I'm some city snob, anyway, so why am I even worrying about it."

Driving home, I felt as if I had had an education of sorts today at my grandfather's side. His writings provided me with insight about himself that I would not have received any other way, whether or not that was ever his intent. Even as a young man, he voiced a keen perspective and insight into the mysteries and beauties of life, and I was benefiting from it. But his words also made me see how little I knew about life at this point. I had been working at a constant frantic pace for years, never allowing my mind to wander to anything else and, for once in my life, I felt strangely shallow. Although I am twice as old as my grandfather was at this point in his journals, he demonstrated an emotional depth that I have yet to achieve. I didn't know whether to feel in awe of him or ashamed of me. Maybe both would be appropriate.

If nothing else on this trip, I would be more aware of the little things about life I had forgotten about…that there are other things in the world beyond my corner office and title. The trouble with being censured by my job was that it had taken away a big part of who I was, and for the past day or so I had felt very lost. But the little bit of grounding I had received from reading a few of my grandfather's journals was already going a long way. Even at a young age, my grandfather had a way of looking at a difficult situation and seeing how he could make it work to his advantage, instead of dwelling on his misfortune. That was a lesson I needed to learn to apply. If I absolutely had to, maybe I could go somewhere else and start all over again, I reasoned in a Jack Bailey sort-of-way. Not the most desired option, but a doable one, and it DID represent an option. I didn't dwell long on that thought however, as at that moment it scared me more than it inspired me. But it did lift my spirits as it gave me a little bit of control. And that was enough for me to consider today a victory of sorts.

The eastern facing light of the setting sun illuminated the maples up ahead, and it reminded me how beautiful this area could be. Living in Atlanta, I missed the ability to roll down the windows on any given afternoon and be over-whelmed by fresh, cool mountain air. Atlanta provides its own potpourri of car exhaust, restaurant aromas, and various other man-made things, but it's not the same as the air of Tennessee. I rolled down the windows and let the breeze fill the cockpit of the car as I traveled the winding country lane. In my mind I became the 17 year old in the '76 red Camaro from so many years ago, riding down the road without a care in the world.

Before I knew it, I was at the farm. There was no sign of the dog as I drove up, which was good as I had forgotten to buy dog food, so I unloaded my car and headed into the house. When I left this morning I was wondering what I would fill my time with in the evenings, missing all the tools of modern technology like cable TV and high speed internet. But now that I knew there were so many journals, so many pieces of wonderful history recorded by my grandfather, I wondered if I could read them all before I had to leave.

I was starving, but the can of spaghetti and bag of rolls I had picked up the night before did not sound overly appealing. Our mothers put the strangest things in our minds when we are little, and one of my brain wrinkles was that you should never waste food. You need to eat what you have before you get anything else. Fortunately, or unfortu-nately, I was miles from the nearest fast food place and was not in the mood to venture out on the suicidal, possum-infested, two-lane roads full of screaming freaks for the sake of a burger and fries. Besides, the six-pack of beer I had picked up along with my other groceries would help alleviate my disappointment a bit. So, spaghetti it would be.

I located a relatively clean pot and began heating the spaghetti on the stove top. With no microwave, everything would take a bit longer than usual...for me, anyway. The rolls were fine as they were as I didn't have the patience for the oven to preheat and then wait for the bread to warm. Reaching into the refrigerator, I pulled out an ice-cold beer and hoped there was a bottle opener somewhere in the house. Luckily, there was.

With a beer in hand and a serving of Chef-Boy-R-Dee's finest warming on the stove top, I walked to the back door in search of my new four-legged friend. She was not to be found, but the view was well worth the trip. Open pasture stretched out below the back yard, creating a private valley all its own, and I could actually hear the wind blowing through the grove of spruce trees in the upper corner of the yard. Otherwise there was complete silence and I wondered whether my long-ago relatives had considered characteristics like these when they chose this as their home. Peace and beauty were probably standard features of every plot of land they found, I reasoned. It was the intangibles like potable water, plowable land, and the lack of wild bear that probably caught their eye.

The spaghetti was starting to make a noise that I didn't think it should be, so I rushed over to pull it off the eye and stir it around to keep it from burning. It seemed plenty warm so I dumped it into a reasonably clean, large, white bowl, and with the bag of rolls in hand and a fresh beer for accompaniment, I made my way back to the living room. It wasn't my house, but considering the circumstances, I didn't think anyone would care if I ate in the living room instead of the kitchen.

After dinner, I lay back on the sofa and took another look

around the large room. With the curtains pulled back and natural light illuminating the darkness of the corners and the shadows from the heavy furniture, the room was not near as dreary to me as when I had arrived the night before. The opening and closing of the doors had let in enough fresh air that the staleness had mostly dissipated...or maybe I had just become accustomed to it. Overall, it wasn't that bad of a place to be. I guess I could survive the week after all.

Jessica opened the door to the house and felt a chill wash over her. Wow, guess I better start setting the heat in the mornings before I go to work, she scolded herself. Though the mountain mornings were cool, the daytime temps didn't seem to warrant setting the heat. But as the days grew shorter and the calendar went deeper into autumn, it could mean the difference between comfort and cold at the end of a long day. Maybe a digital thermostat with autotimer should be next on her ever-changing list of house projects.

The house was the one her mother had lived in before she died. When it became Jessica's, she put a significant amount of money and sweat equity into making sure it had the touches and amenities she had become accustomed to in her old life. Some of them made life easier, some of them were purely indulgent, and she had installed most of them. The only things she had needed professional help for were electrical and plumbing...and that was only from a lack of time to learn the fundamentals of wiring and water.

She flipped on the light and looked toward the answering machine. One flash. Another flash. One flash. Another flash. Two messages. Flipping the switch, the tape rewound and, after the cursory beep, her mother's sister's voice came on.

"Jessica, it's Betty. I haven't heard from you in days, dear, and I'm just a little worried, that's all." You're always worried, Aunt Betty, nothing new. "Just give me a call when you can. I love you!" Betty was Jessica's last living blood family and she lived about 60 miles away in Kingsport.

Beep.

"Jessica, it's Brian. Listen, I don't know if you even thought any more about my offer last week, but I really hope you'll give it some serious consideration. I know you've been wanting to head up north to see the leaves change, and maybe this would be a good time for us to talk...just a suggestion, but...anyway, just wanted to check in with you."

Her finger hovered over the delete key on the second message before giving in. Brian was her old boss from Washington, D.C., and for the past few months, he had put together an attractive deal to try and entice her back into the business. It was something she could at least consider, she told herself. Consideration would either open her eyes to a chapter in her life she was willing to reopen, or it would solidify that she was where she wanted to be, doing what she wanted to be doing. She had been deeply hurt in that chapter of her life, and she wasn't one who let go of hurt easily. But she couldn't carry a grudge forever. Either way, it was a decision for another day as today had just been horrible.

It was as if 12 hours worth of work was shoved into her 8-hour schedule. Ms. Weldin had decided Jessica was the devil trying to take her soul when she went in to give her blood pressure medication, and had showered Jessica with the remainder of pureed mixed vegetables from her lunch tray. Ms. Weldin suffered from dementia, among other things, and it seemed things were becoming more and more disconnected for her. Mr. Weems had 'inadvertently' caused his bedpan to leak on the bed, requiring a complete cleaning of his genitals and a change of his sheets and egg crate. As this was the third 'accident' in the past two weeks, she was beginning to wonder if he was simply looking for a cheap thrill. Finally, Mrs. Humphries, the chronic complainer, spent twenty minutes chastising Jessica about there being too much light in her room when she was trying to sleep at four o'clock in the afternoon. Though Sweet Branch had invested in updated window coverings during recent months, this was not the Hilton and light DID peek through western-facing rooms late in the day. She had promised to look into it for Mrs. Humphries, but she fully expected another equally serious complaint coming her way tomorrow.

After a day like this, a hot steaming shower seemed like a temptation Jessica could not resist. She kicked off her shoes and began undressing on the way to her master bathroom. A line of clothes followed her down the entryway, through the bedroom, and into the large adjoining bathroom. Maybe she'd get a chance to clean up the place later this week, but after a day like today, that was not a priority.

Jessica turned on the vanity light and stared at the person looking back at her. She had no clue what Carter Lee was having to look at so late in the day and was somewhat relived to see she didn't look as badly as she feared. Turning the shower on to hot, she arranged her towels on the counter and pulled out her ponytail holder as steam began to fill the open bathroom. She checked the water temperature and, as she turned her head from the spray of the water, she caught a glimpse of her nude figure in the long dressing mirror on the back of the bathroom door. Her late thirties figure was not unattractive, in fact quite pleasing. For whatever reason, all the women in her family had been blessed with figures that somehow took care of themselves, requiring little maintenance in the form of silly workout routines or long distance running. As long as she kept the diet reasonable and didn't vegetate on the sofa for weeks at a time, her figure kept the extra weight at bay and subtly defined the curves of her slender frame. Her long auburn hair fell just above her breasts and framed a defined face and deep green eyes.

Feeling relieved that she was not completely dishhelved, but only moderately frumpy, she held her hand under the water of the rain dance shower head until the temperature was as she wanted, then climbed in. The moist warmth of the onrushing stream slowly soaked her hair and cascaded down the length of her long body, taking the day with it. She drenched a washcloth in the cleansing torrent and softly pressed it against her face, massaging her eyes in slow circles as she went. As the water released her tensions, she leaned against the side of the shower and let the water massage her body.

Jessica started thinking about the message from Brian on her machine. She didn't know what bothered her more: what he had allowed to happen all those years ago, or how it seemed he was now trying to make up for it. It felt like, for lack of a better description, a bribe to make his still-guilty conscience feel better. Single incidents can change a person's perception in the eyes of another, and Brian wasn't the pillar of values he had been to her in the past. Sad, she thought. There had been times when Jessica wondered if she was simply too idealistic for the reality of equity and finance, but then she would remind herself that it's not unrealistic to want someone you can believe in, no matter the industry.

Maybe it might be a good idea to take some time off, she thought, and return to D.C. to visit. There were hatchets to bury and opportunities to investigate, and a change of scenery might reinvigorate her. While she loved what she did and had not felt a pang of regret since changing her career and moving to Tennessee, it WAS a taxing profession. Death was a constant coworker and despite her vast reservoir of compassion and the ability to put herself in the place of so many families hurting for their dying loved one, it cast a shadow on her mood from time-to-time.

Flipping off the shower, she wrapped her hair in a towel, pulled on a heavy old terry cloth robe and cinched it tight around her waist. The house had begun to warm up, but a slight chill still lingered, so adding her moccasin slippers to her current attire would be a good touch. It was only early October, but the nights in the Tennessee mountains cooled substantially this time of year. She often went to work wearing a sweater, only to come home in short sleeves. It could be annoying at times. But the seasons held a special place in Jessica's heart, for they signaled change, even if everything else in her life stayed constant. Her mood felt lighter in the cooling autumn, and even if only her perception, she felt other's burdens lightened a touch at this time of year as well.

Jessica decided to check how the stock market had performed today before doing anything else. She had always had a keen interest in money and markets and it was one thing that had drawn her to her old career. Several of the people she worked with on private equity projects had some of the sharpest financial minds she had ever encountered. Though she was no slouch when it came to mathematics and investing, the ability of these people to take a convoluted mixture of financial data and immediately understand the financial benefits, risks, and hedging strategies of a potential acquisition was uncanny. She had not hesitated to take any advice or insight they offered when it came to money management and long term investing, and she was still benefiting from their words of wisdom.

Over the years, she had built up quite a nest egg from nothing and become more and more confident in her own blend of equity, debt, and hedging strategies to grow her money while protecting her principal. Her promotions at the firm and participation in bonuses for the deals and opportunities she consulted on helped buoy the account balance well into the high six-figures. When she inherited the small estate her mother had left her, she immediately put the money to work and now enjoyed a monthly cash flow from her portfolio that allowed her to use her nursing salary as fun money. In true Cooper fashion, however, she continued to split all her funds between saving, spending on necessities, and giving to charities and individuals who had needs greater than her own. No one, not even her coworkers, would have known she had a liquid net worth of over $1,000,000.

In her mother's old spare bedroom she had set up the quintessential home office. Though her new vocation didn't require an office environment, it was a characteristic of her old life that she truly missed. When cable internet had finally become available in the area she was the first one to sign-up, and even took a day off of work in order to not miss the installer. Once in place, she immediately ordered a completely new, top of the line computer with all the latest accessories and technologically advanced gadgets. The room itself underwent a transformation from carpet, white walls, and a single overhead light to light oak hardwoods, fresh paint, wainscoting and crown molding on the walls, and a six-pack of recessed lighting in the ceiling. Once the integrated set of light wood desk and bookcases arrived via tractor trailer from IKEA, the transformation was complete.

The computer was up and running in no time and when her browser flashed its familiar 'Welcome to Your Yahoo Page,' she flipped immediately to her brokerage account to check her stocks. Overall, the market had a healthy move for the day and her portfolio was faring even better. There was one position she had failed to hedge yesterday and luckily it had not cost her anything today. In fact, MacHillock Technologies was up half a point. Once she had an idea which way MacHillock's longer-term momentum was going to take it, she would revisit her hedging strategy. Until then, she didn't have to worry about it. She was preparing to get up and begin dinner when an impulsive thought flashed across her mind.

Google Carter Lee.

Oh, now that's just plain silly, she thought to herself. Carter Lee was of no more interest to her than any other family member who came to the facility. Granted, there weren't many men her age who visited the facility on a regular basis, much less single men with piercing blue eyes and a swagger of confidence that caught her attention. OK, maybe he did interest her more than she was willing to let on, but she didn't know any more about him than his name, place of residence, and that he was Jack Bailey's grandson.

All the more reason to see if there is anything about him worth knowing, she heard herself reason.

Point taken, self.

She pointed her browser to www.google.com and tried 'carter lee accountant atlanta.'

Jessica looked at the list of entries and, before settling in for her research on Carter Lee, removed the towel from her drying hair and went to the kitchen for a glass of wine. She felt wonderfully content at this moment; warm in her robe and slippers, sipping wine, and entering the portal of information unending in its possibilities.

Jessica scanned the hits as they ran down the page.

"Atlanta Georgia CPA Firm, Atlanta Thrashers, HAWKS Staff Directory, Atlanta Accountants, Southeast Conference on College Cost Accounting. Hmmmmm. I don't recall him talking about sports management."

Jessica tried more general parameters this time.

'carter lee atlanta'

The first hit read: Carter Lee, Executive Biography, Associated Media Limited.

She clicked the link and up popped a picture of the man she had met at the Sweet Branch facility today who passed himself off as an accountant.

"Accountant my behind..." she muttered as his full page biography filled the screen.

Carter Lee has served as a primary champion of the Associated Media Limited mission, guiding several of the company's key ventures during a period of unprecedented growth and dedicating his efforts to securing the company's recognition as one of the most respected organizations in the world. Lee serves the company as Sr. Vice President of Global Development and Acquisitions. He and his team identify opportunities for the company to expand and build on its role as an industry leader. He also directs the global coordination and execution of organic growth opportunities, providing a single point of access to potential joint ventures and new opportunity partners of Associated Media Limited.

Since joining Associated Media Limited in 1992, Lee has held management positions in a host of AML subsidiaries. Associated Media Limited has twice recognized him with its Five Star Award, the company's highest honor, in appreciation of his outstanding leadership.Lee serves on the board of directors for Youth Programs Inc. and the United Way of the South. He is also a board member of Southern Services Corporation. A native of Tennessee, Lee earned his bachelor's degree from Duke University and an International MBA from the University of South Carolina. He also served in the United States Navy for four years, rising to the rank of Lieutenant.

Aren't you a surprise, she thought as she studied the hi-resolution image of Carter Lee, corporate executive. She didn't know of him specifically, but she knew about Associated Media Limited. Jessica had invested quite a large amount in their stock about a year ago. At about the same time, Associated Media announced a deal that the market hated and the stock priced dropped substantially. It stayed low for most of the year and caused her a good bit of worry as she hated even the possibility of losing money. She eventually made a nice profit on the whole deal, but never invested in Associated Media again.

I may have to give him a hard time about that deal if I get the chance, she thought.

The picture on his profile must have been a few years old since the man she met today had a touch of gray starting, whereas the man in the picture still had a full head of deep brown hair. The face, however, was the same one that caught her eye early this morning. A slender face, flanked by hard lines of the jaw and chin, accented with the unforgettable blue eyes. No doubt existed in her mind that this was the same man. But why had he lied about what he did? It's one thing to stretch the truth to the upside, saying you're more than you really are; he had done the complete opposite...reducing himself to nothing more than a staff position. Maybe he was ashamed of what he did...or maybe he was just losing his connection to it. She had experienced that once, and it had changed her life completely. She could still recall the events of that day years ago...her 'tipping point' of sorts.

She recalled staring out the window of her D.C. office, 8 stories above the street below. Her head pounded with the ache of ceaseless meetings that began the moment she walked in that cool November morning, and wound down just as the clock approached 6:00 p.m.

So much for crossing anything off my to-do list today, she smirked to herself, half in amusement yet part in frustration. It had been an easy transition at first, a new opportunity and a stronger position, but it appeared that after six months, the honeymoon period of her newly-granted promotion was approaching its end. Hackson and Webley was one of the best firms on the East Coast, and selective was a description that accurately described its willingness to take on new consultants, much less one without an Ivy League sheepskin. But she came from a long line of determined people who 'didn't use the front door,' as her dad liked to say, and she smiled at the memory of his words.

She stared at the long list of uncompleted items on the page and sighed. With all I've NOT accomplished today, I might as well just call it a day and knock it all out tomorrow, she thought to herself. She put her cup back in its familiar place and stood up to switch off her computer. Jessica disconnected the laptop from the unit and placed it in the carrying case flipped open on her back desk. As she turned to leave, she suddenly felt the presence of someone nearby.

"Brian! You startled me," she snapped, her mood relaying the grayness of the day.

"Sorry, Jessica, I didn't mean to." He paused, the normally carefree Brian looking uncharacteristically uneasy. He had been one of the few she connected with from the beginning of her employment at H & W. But with Brian being the person she reported to, distance was the norm and their friendship was limited by necessity.

"Can I come in? I haven't felt good about our last conversation."

"Yes, please come in." You aren't the only one, she thought.

Brian eased in and shut the door. He slowly pulled up the chair, never taking his eyes off of hers.

"I'm worried about how you interpreted the whole situation with Debrini. I don't think you fully understand it all."

"How SHOULD I have interpreted that, Brian?" The words shot out of her before she could stop them. "I have worked for weeks on the Debrini deal and suddenly all that is for naught? I'm told to hand it off without any explanation. It's one thing to hand off something when my resources are needed on something better, but to have my time and effort go to the benefit of someone else for…well…for what I can only perceive to be a questionable reason is a bit disconcerting."

"I'm sorry, Jessica….it's not my choice. I want you to know that. I think you've been a fantastic addition to this place, and since you've been here, it's really added a dimension that—"

"Don't patronize me, Brian. I've put everything I've had into this job ever since I was promoted and if I've screwed up, well…" She paused and waited.

Brian sighed. "Jessica, I wish it were that. Mr. Debrini is…well…somewhat old fashioned. He doesn't have a problem with your work; it's just that he is more comfortable with…with…well…with a man."

She felt a numbness wash over her hands, still clasped to her black computer bag. This was the 2000s. This was supposed to be a world where we did not judge our peers by the bathroom door they entered or the heritage of their family, but by what they contributed in shared circumstances. All her life that had been one of her core beliefs; to be open to the person who was inside, not the external packaging. Yet here she was, her contributions now reduced to a denotation of her gender; without recourse, without examination.

"You're not serious…" she whispered, gripping the handle in her hand even tighter. "Did you reason with him?"

Brian ignored her question. "It makes me sick, Jessica, but please understand…Mr. Debrini is a very close friend of Webley, and I'm afraid the client's desire, however asinine it might be, took precedent, and…" his voice drifted off, embarrassed by what he was saying, yet compelled to say something, no matter how devoid of sense it seemed.

"Who gets the client now?" she asked, her eyes drifting down to the large accordion file that she filled with several completed documents late last night.

"Thompson...Ed Thompson."

She felt her normally dancing green eyes cloud up in a perilous squint.

"Ed?"

"Ed." Brian knew that he had just doused an ember with gasoline, and not knowing quite what to do next, he stood up. He looked at his watch, hoping to look purposeful, while feeling quite lost in the entire moment.

"Jessica, I know you've worked long and hard for this client and that the hardest part is already complete, thanks to you..."

Just in time to make Thompson look like a bloody genius, Jessica wanted to scream.

"And while that is out of both of our control, I want to do something for you that, quite frankly, I'm not sure I have the authority to do. I want to send you on a paid getaway for the weekend, on the firm." He knew his words sounded like a feeble attempt at regaining whatever remained of his masculinity, but it was all he could think of to offer. "Why don't I just let that soak in for a little while...something tells me I've said enough in the past few minutes..." He looked at her face, and slowly his eyes drifted down like a chastised schoolboy as he turned to leave. He paused once more without looking back, hoping for any type of request to return, then continued on.

Jessica felt the end of her mouth curling up in a twisted grin. You can always tell a man who's married...he senses when to shut up, she thought.

She pulled her coat off the door and took one last look around, her eye catching the large leather-bound file on her desk, now a symbol of prejudice instead of the pride she wanted it to be. As she closed the door, she remembered she had forgotten to turn off the light. Oh, well...guess that will just have to come out of H & W's profits this year, she bemused, and accented the thought by slamming the door.

The November night met her faithfully as she exited the revolving door. Thompson, she fumed, taking deep breaths as she pounded the sidewalk. Head bowed, she dared the sidewalk population to cross her path. Of all people, Jessica seethed. She wanted to be so good, so caring...a person that, irrespective of what anyone else thought, she could feel proud of herself for giving the best she could and finding the best in others. With Ed Thompson, the latter had failed. In their first meeting, she had sensed that their planets were just not in alignment, and that, somehow, he would be an ever present body blocking her light. It wasn't just one thing about Ed Thompson that annoyed her, it was all of him. It was his deceit with clients who unknowingly became the objects of ridicule seconds upon their exit from the office. It was his annoying propensity for stating the obvious, and the cockiness resulting from sharing this with the world. It was his smug way of looking at her across the conference table and communicating how silly and mundane he thought her suggestions were—even though they were usually the most effective.

She wanted to scream. She wanted to give him AND Brian a good, hard shaking and relay to them, in no uncertain terms, what she thought about their 'good old boy' system. Jessica felt her frustration peaking, slowly giving way to what she knew she really felt. Hurt. She could mask it and cry foul to the audience of the world, but after all was done, what would remain was that empty feeling of being minimized into nothing, and there was nothing she could do about it.

Why do I let people like that get to me, she wondered. It's not like little Ed could ever compete with me on equal ground. She smiled, then laughed, at her own viciousness. It was so out of character for her to be so mean—yet very comforting—despite being a majority of one.

"Oh, well...Ed can compare parts with old Mr. Debrini to his heart's content now," she muttered to herself. "I'll find other places to put my energy."

As fate would have it, it was that same night that her mother called to break the news that her cancer was terminal. At the most, she had four, maybe six months, left. Though Jessica had put years into her career and her success, the combination of her mother's condition and the way in which she had been professionally reduced to a set of genitalia made the decision to cash out and leave a very easy one. In her mind, this would not be permanent. At some point, she would reenter the profession, but on her own terms and with a firm SHE wanted as much as it would want her.

But she never did return. After her mother died, she realized that caring for her mother in her last days had given her a sense of completeness, as if her natural abilities had finally found an outlet to showcase themselves. Alone, yet financially secure, she made the decision that she had more to offer herself and the world than just some financial advice and a bill rate. Jessica entered a transitional nursing program at a local university that allowed her to focus solely on the training she needed to become a full-fledged registered nurse. And for the past several years, that was her life...being the hands of care for people who might not know the care of another human being, if not for her. If she was honest with herself, she didn't miss her old life one bit, and felt a little sorry for those who still devoted everything to goals that only benefited a few.

"Good luck with all that, Mr. Lee. I hope you find your happiness there." She sighed and headed to the kitchen to reheat the remainder of the dinner from last night.

After a quick rest on the sofa, I grabbed another beer and began exploring the living area with a bit more interest than I had the night before. My quest was to both satisfy my curiosity about the particulars of my grandfather's life, and have something even remotely interesting to do. The lack of free time is a situation lamented by many in today's age, but when one doesn't have anything productive to fill a block of free time with, it's not the blessing many would think.

When I was young and my parents and I would visit my grandparents, the first part of the conversation would be about me. What I did in school, who my friends were, what I got for my birthday, etc., etc. Slowly, however, the topics would turn to more grown-up topics such as other family members, topics in the news, and speculation on this and that. I would then be able to slowly reconnoiter the room, taking in each knick-knack, picture, and strange object I could to pass the time before we went back home.

Years later, I found myself in the very same situation, only this time I was free to touch, inspect, and look at anything I pleased. Knick-knacks from long forgotten trips still sat in the very place they were first positioned long ago…the dust-free areas underneath most of them giving away their secret. Pictures of people of varying ages dotted the tabletops and side tables. I guess everyone populates their space with items that have special meaning to them; however, without them there to translate, the meanings are lost and the items become just another piece of clutter.

I finally made it to the wide desk from which I took several of my grandfather's journals before rushing out the door this morning. There wasn't room for much else on the desk, but in the upper corner I noticed a picture of a dog that was very similar in look to the one I had encountered earlier this morning. It could not be of the dog from this morning however, as this was an older picture, likely taken back when black and white photography was the common standard. The frame was of a heavy black metal made to resemble vines that interwove, forming a tight mesh. The weight and solid feel of the frame put modern day frames of aluminum and other weak metals to shame. You got your money's worth back then, I thought to myself.

I turned it over to see how the picture went into the frame and noticed a white label of some type on the back with the words 'Patch 4/1948.' As I returned the picture to the desk, I was wishing that someone had written the breed of dog on the picture frame, as well.

Pretty breed, whatever it is.

Aside from a coffee cup serving as a pencil holder, a very old scotch tape dispenser, and a pile of old legal pads, the only thing left on the desk were the journals. I speculated that the journals on the left side must be from early in my grandfather's life; the ones to the right the latter part of his life. This would make sense as the ones I had pulled from the left side of the desk today started in 1939, when my grandfather would have been in his twenties. On top of the most recent pile of journals sat a new, metal-ringed binder that appeared to be the most recent addition to the collection. I had not noticed it before, but now it seemed oddly out of place. It was more of a notebook than a journal, as if the same person who had taken such pains to only buy quality, lasting journals had not felt the same need to be as picky with this one. Curious, I opened the cover to find pages from a yellow legal pad filled with my grandfather's handwriting inside. The pages had been three-hole punched to fit the notebook, but aside from reading the contents, there were no other clues as to why this varied so drastically from the rest. Since I was at the end of my exploration of the living area and was not interested, or brave enough, to explore all the dark rooms of the 100+ year old farmhouse by myself, I decided I would close the night out at least understanding what this little binder may hold. I lay down on the couch and, with a pillow underneath my side for support, focused on the first page in the binder. I listened as my grandfather's words began to speak.

A week ago I came to grips with the fact that I'm dying. We're all dying, of course, but I am at the stage of life where I have a reasonably finite period in which my life will end. Within the next six months or so, the living, breathing, thinking, feeling entity that is me will cease to exist upon this Earth. No more me. I don't quite know how I feel about it yet. On one hand, there is the sadness of knowing that there will be many people, places, and things I will never get to see again, or never have the chance to experience at all. On the other hand, there is an element of relief, a feeling that the long laborious journey that has been my life will be winding down, and I will soon be in the presence of Almighty God. It's a confusing mix of feelings—regret tinged with relief and anticipation.

Many in my situation may feverishly make a list of all the things they want to accomplish before moving on. Young people especially may feel the need to capture as much satisfaction from what they may view as a short-changed situation, a raw deal that brought early closure to a life still full of potential and promise. I, however, am not of that population. If anything, I'm receiving what my 87 year old life is due—closure. At my age, death is more of an expectation, the only surprise being the exact moment of its arrival. As I mentioned, I think I have a range now...a general idea of when my final visitor will knock on the door of my soul and tell me we're going home.

Faced with this situation, I pondered for several days what I should do. I'd feel stupid sitting in a chair, rotting away like I was waiting for a bus. It wouldn't be unreasonable, but it would be boring to say the least. I'm dying, but I'm not dead...yet. I need something meaningful to do for closure. Then

I remembered my journals—years and years of journals, locked away in a box in the attic. For most of my adult life, I have kept simple journals of my trek through time. They are nothing that would rival the journals of Thoreau or Aristotle, but they are invaluable to me. Written recollections of forgotten memories and emotions which cover decades of history. My history. I began keeping journals when I was 20, mainly out of necessity as my memory has never been one to brag about. Into these leather-bound satchels of parchment would go the typical stray thoughts, ideas, and dreams that cross a man's mind over the course of his life. All men have dreams, mine just happen to have gained longevity from the function of paper and pen. It was time to reflect on what my life's eye had seen...and what I had really been about.

To find my journals, my neighbor agreed to rummage through the boxes and boxes of God knows what in our attic that stuck to my late wife and I like magnets over the years. Funny how you really have no specific idea what you have in attics, basements, and the like, but know just enough to find some semblance of value in it that warrants not throwing it out. I was hopeful that the journals had persevered enough to stick around to take me on a journey back in time.

Down from the attic came a pathetic, dusty, brown box, its sides reinforced by multiple administrations and colors of tape and other adhesives to keep it together for just one more year. But one more year it would not take, and with a loud 'thunk,' the box hit the hardwood floor and spilled forth a lifetime of leather caretakers. There they were—the historians of time that held the power to make me young again...for a little while, anyway.

The man stood and looked at the pile and then looked at me, half curious and half incredulous of this new project I had decided to take on at my advanced age. When I asked him to find my journals, he apparently was thinking of two, maybe three, small notebooks. Not sixty-seven or so.

We took the now disarrayed journals and piled them neatly one-by-one on the desk in the living room. Considering their age and wear, the journals had fared surprisingly well. Most seemed to be well intact, with only the occasional torn spine or wrinkled page indicating any activity other than resting quietly for years in a sweltering attic. For whatever reason, I had developed a habit early on of writing the date a journal started on the inside page and the ending date on the last page, so I mouthed a quiet 'thank you' to the me of years ago for making the task of sorting them much easier. I wanted an accurate flow of time, from youth to old age, from ignorance to wisdom, and all points in-between. It would read better, I thought, and give me the picture of life I longed to recall.

After all had been arranged, my neighbor stood back and took in the scene of this frail old man and his piles of life narratives. Rarely has he been absent of a voiced opinion, but on this evening, he simply stood there with his hands on his hips and looked curiously at me, as if I was going to offer an explanation of what I was about to do. But I wasn't. Sometimes you simply don't know what to say because you simply have nothing to say, and that is where I found myself. As did he. So two generations of men mumbled awkwardly in an awkward moment and with a brief handshake, parted company for the night.

I looked at this pile of paper, leather, and metal and wondered for a moment if I would live long enough to read it all. Or if I would want to read it all. I found myself a little apprehensive, almost frightened, at the concept of revisiting my entire life in print. What had I forgotten? What memories that I treasured today maybe did not happen quite the way I thought they did? And did the good outweigh the bad? Did I want to color the very last days of my life with sorrow, sadness, and regret if that indeed was what lay before me in this litany of information? Troubling.

More troubling, though, would be the angst of NOT knowing. Not remembering. Not reliving. Though I knew there would be some pain from it, the reanimation of my history would give me a full life perspective that few of us get to have. At this stage of my life, I figured I was hedged pretty well. If revisiting the past caused me pain, it would not be for very long...six months at the most. But if it gave me joy, I would pass away content and ready to move to the next life. No downside.

I went to the first journal on the stack nearest to me...the oldest one...and took the first journal from its place. I sat down in my chair under my reading light and cleaned my glasses with a soft cloth. Slowly I turned through the pages, smelling the scent of the leather and the parchment, noting each stray mark, nick, and notation on the pages. I reopened the journal to the first page and began reading the first entry: 'Today is April 5, 1939. It's a cool day here, but the ground is already showing the promise of the coming spring. We're itching to get the crops in the ground. The Farmer's Almanac says this will be an early spring and...' I felt my mind slipping away to a simpler time. The twenty year old me of yesterday was reaching out to the dying me of today in words that were solid, confident, and clear. I felt my age as I heard the confidence of this young man radiating across the eons of time that separated us. There is so much we must discuss, I thought to myself. There is so much I need to know...to recall...to remember.

I read and re-read for a solid week, stopping only for food, medicine, personal needs and, of course, sleep. One blessing of old age is that you don't need as much sleep as when you are younger, so the quiet hours when the world slumbers afforded me the perfect opportunity to continue my quest. And what a quest it was. Through the pages of my journals I traveled roads, visited friends, and laughed as I had not laughed in years. Apparitions of memories now materialized in full form...both the good and the bad.

In one moment I marveled at my selflessness, only to cringe at my cruelty the next. You see all parts of yourself when you *undertake an exercise like this. You see decisions that make you look like a genius, followed by decisions that prove you are the biggest idiot who ever lived. You see how badly you hurt people when you didn't mean to, and you see the blessings you sometimes brought to someone without even the hint of intent. I learned that I still have a lot to learn…even now.*

Finally I was done. I was exhausted. I was spent. But I felt more alive than I had in years, and I was bursting with the need to capture what I had just experienced into one last journal. One last narrative. One final goodbye. In a matter of hours I went from reader to writer, fearful of wasting even a moment that I had left. I lived a range of emotions this past week…from utter desolation to exceeding joy…and everything in-between. I now understand that the interconnectivity of the events in one's life is much more complex than any of us realize. Your choice of career, for example, can lead you to a certain job in a certain city where it just so happens that your soulmate resides. The one you will spend your life with. You may think, 'I am so fortunate to have accepted THAT job with THAT company which brought me to THAT city where I met THAT person.' But is that what really happened? What if, just for sake of argument, it wasn't your job that drove the events, but instead the subconscious draw of this person that caused everything else to fall into place? What if you unconsciously knew THEY were the one, and THEY lived in THAT city, and THAT company had an office in THAT city and THAT company just happened to make you a job offer. What if…

But it's not my intent to wallow down a rabbit hole of hypothesis and conjecture but instead, to share in the most honest and simple of ways, what I have seen at this point. What seems to matter…and what seems to last. It's taken me a long time to become the person I am and, if I'm honest with myself, I could have done a few things differently.

Standing at the end of the trail and looking back over my journey, it's quite clear to me that my life was composed of very distinct events that were all underwritten by one constant: love. Even each of our lives, the complete containment of everything we are and everything we hope to be, was conceived from an act of love. It's not that my work and other similar life obligations weren't important to me; they were. They simply weren't the memories of my life that my heart recalled. Making a living is not the same thing as making a life—the former is only a means to an end. We mislead ourselves when we believe credentials on the wall or money in the bank can replace love in our lives. Our hearts know the truth.

I also learned that pain had an incredible impact on my life and my memories. It's not that I suffered—I've learned that in this world I'm not the only one who is called to bear disappointments; there are countless others who are in a far worse plight. But there were very vivid recollections of disappointment, of loss, of despair, that impacted me so deeply I recorded them in great detail over the years. Those moments touch my heart even now, but they also served as balance for the moments of joy, happiness, and contentment that I was so blessed to share. Just as we cannot hate one we have never loved, it is equally hard to fully appreciate the gift of joy unless we have suffered the anguish of disappointment or sadness. Otherwise, we have nothing against which we can compare.

Life doesn't give us very many second chances, if it ever gives any at all. But when it does, we should take full advantage of it without thinking twice. And that is what I will do now as I feel compelled to capture it all in writing...before I lose my chance. God has his reasons for things, so who am I to question Him about why I'm doing what I'm doing. I just want you to know that—

And then it stopped, halfway down the page, as if something else had caught his attention and he never returned to finish his thought. Directly below his ending were date ranges and numbers that didn't make any sense to me. I flipped to the next page to see if he had simply continued on a new page, but the first few lines of that page indicated a completely new topic. I was too tired to start a new narrative tonight, so I closed the binder and placed it in my backpack. With no obvious rhyme or reason as to what he intended with either his abrupt ending or cryptic table of numbers, I was left grappling for closure.

Know what? I wondered to myself as I moved the pillow from under my shoulder to behind my head. There is only one other person in this world who could leave me hanging this way. I guess you definitely are my mother's father.

As Carter let the full meal, three bottles of beer, and reading take affect, he realized that he had not thought about work for the past several hours. It was unlike him to not dwell on topics of work for that long a period of time. If anything, it was the only topic that had truly occupied most of the minutes of his life for the past several years.

The realization and reminder of his work brought back all the memories, thoughts, and fears of the past twenty-four hours, and he felt those dark uncertain feelings wash back over him again. What would become of him after all this? Yes, Mike had told him he was an excellent performer, but who tells excellent performers to go away for a week? Did the Bulls give Michael Jordan a sabbatical in the middle of their championship season? Was Bill Gates ice-fishing all winter when Microsoft was in its heyday? Was James Cameron told to take a few weeks off right in the middle of filming Titanic? No, no and no, he told himself, and no one would ask me to go away if I was that critical to the organization. Carter had argued himself into a position that he was unable to retreat from, so there was nothing left to do but stare blankly into space. What would become of me, he wondered, if they didn't need…or want…me any longer.

He could always find another job with a bigger title and higher compensation, but it would mean having to start all over again. Proving himself. Building relationships. Figuring out who to know and who to avoid. What the important people want and don't want. What he could get away with and what he couldn't. All of that discovery takes effort, and in some ways he doubted if he could even establish himself like that again. It was so tiring and even...pointless.

Coming back here had awakened some things in him he thought were gone for good. Maybe small animals did scamper here and there on a quest to try and kill him, and maybe his car was a bit pretentious for an area populated largely with Ford and Chevy pickups, but in the past 24 hours he had found himself with a new breath of life...of awareness...and interests. He couldn't recall the last time he had looked at an open field and been genuinely impressed by how beautifully it lay. No ornate landscaping; no sculpted gardens or winding river rock paths to decorate it. Just a simple portrait of how things naturally arise and exist without any help from man.

And the nurse who was taking care of his grandfather. Jessica. She had awakened something else in him that he had not felt for quite some time. When he first arrived at the hospice center, he had viewed her as just another competent female professional who could assist him in finding his grandfather amongst the lines and lines of patient rooms. In fact, she did not seem very interested in being in his presence and, at the time, he really didn't care. He didn't want to be there to begin with.

But later in the day, as he was watching her attend to his grandfather, he found he was watching her with much more than just an interest in patient care. At least in the physical sense, she embodied so much that he found attractive in a woman, but for years had completely ignored in the pursuit of his career. The lines of her face and the richness of her eyes drew his gaze, and there was more than one time he knew she caught him looking more at her than what she was doing for her patient. From time-to-time she would casually take her hand and move her ponytail to whichever side was to her advantage, exposing the gentle curve where the line of her shoulder and neck came together. Even the very nature of her caring for other people moved him. There was so much more in the world that could be more glamorous or lucrative, yet this was how she chose to make her way in life.

What captured him completely, he realized, was the first time he saw her smile. The sheer embarrassment of his 'possum in the road' fiasco was well worth the benefit of seeing her suddenly aglow with such a captivating smile. Eyes that had been cold to him up to that point now warmed with light, and her gentle laugh complemented her amusement perfectly. A man of 42 may have first made her acquaintance, but a young 17 year old just touching the edge of a crush bid her goodbye at day's end.

Carter repositioned the pillow and let the full weight of his head rest against it. A numbing feeling washed over him as he felt himself giving way to sleep, without concern over his physical condition or the events of the day. Drifting slowly, his muscles relaxed and gently he let sleep take hold.

He felt the breeze in his hair and the streams of sunlight washing across his face. Opening his eyes, the brightness of the sun limited his ability to see, and he felt completely detached from any particular place. Ethereal, without a body or state of mind, yet his senses were intensely aware. As he became more aware of his surroundings, he found himself in a small glade, encompassed by towering oaks and maples exploding in colors of red, yellow, and brown. In the midst of the glade stood a small sapling, new in growth and looking only recently sprouted. He was standing near the small tree, as if he was its caretaker, and it seemed odd that in a period of decline, new life would begin.

As he raised his head, the intense sunlight that illuminated the area suddenly began to diminish, and a mist crept forth from the edges of the glade, obscuring everything around him. A feeling of fear began to overtake him, and the desire to run grew in his chest. His eyes locked on a portion of the wooded area and a figure, without face or appendage, formed from the mist. It began to take shape, closer to human with each passing moment, until what stood in the mist was the figure of a man—without eyes and without features with which to express emotion. The figure began to move slowly toward him. His heartbeat increased, pounding in his ears, yet he could not turn nor run...he could only watch the form creeping closer and closer to him. It came within inches of him and stopped, as if waiting to be acknowledged. He did not move. Then, what appeared to be a hand moved toward him and gently touched his arm. From deep inside him arose an intense feeling of sadness, consuming any fear he had felt. Suddenly a face appeared, and the mouth formed the words that he heard only in his mind:

"You...must...know..."

It was the face of his grandfather.

Carter awoke with a start. Bolting from the couch, he knocked the beer bottle to the floor creating a carpet of shards. Every muscle and nerve in his body was literally frozen with fear. He stood shaking in the middle of the living room, not knowing where to turn or what to do and unable to control his anxiety. His breath came in rapid bursts, his emotions a mix of fright and adrenaline, and he began to get dizzy.

There is not much that frightens a grown man. But this did, and he was petrified. Terrors that can captivate the mind of a child have no place in the rational mind of an adult. Everything that goes bump in the night has a reason, a justification, an explanation. This experience, however, had none.

The intense nature of it touched him too deeply to be just a simple passing thought. The eyes he had faced in the misty abyss were real...too real to be disregarded as fantasy. He wanted to believe that the unfamiliarity of a strange place, coupled with the stress of the day and the fatigue of the drive, had all combined in some wicked way to take control of his mind. Carter looked around and felt completely out of sync with reality. It was as if every haunting feeling he had ever experienced had been given new life. In one evil union, they joined together to accompany him, to make his feeling of isolation and fear that much more intense.

Sidestepping broken glass, he slowly moved up to the bedroom and lay down with his arm resting on his forehead. Several minutes passed before he felt able enough to sit up, and even then he did not feel well. It was as if his mind and his body were caught in different worlds—one of reality and one of fantasy. Whatever was happening to him, he was not handling it well.

OK, that was interesting, Carter said to himself. He did not allow himself to linger on the image for fear the thought would stay in his mind for much longer than he wanted. If that happened, he would never go to sleep. He shut off the bedside lamp and, foregoing all nighttime rituals, crawled deep into the covers hiding from everything seen and unseen.

It's a long time until daylight, he thought.

WEDNESDAY

Carter spent the next day poring through more of his grandfather's journals, becoming increasingly intimate with Jack Bailey's most private thoughts, hopes, and dreams. These journals were no longer mere reading material to help Carter pass the time. The journals were now a portal into the person he most longed to know; a person whom he never viewed so much as a human being, but as a familial icon whom everyone revered and loved.

Up until now, Jack had been a grandfather largely in title only, but now he was becoming a man who, like Carter himself, had experienced the highs and lows of life. The roads they had traveled were similar in many ways; their views and perceptions of life equally parallel. The only difference was that Jack Bailey had started his journey much earlier.

Toward the end of the day, Carter focused on his grandfather's cryptic outline of dates and numbers contained on the first entry of the yellow pages in the small binder. Jack had drawn a small table that showed three blocks of dates, followed by a number. The dates were chronological and were so wide in range that they could not be pointing to a specific event. It looked like a table of birth and death dates:

1939 – 1953	*1*
1953 – 2001	*2*
2001 – 2006	*3*

That's when it hit him: maybe these were periods in his grandfather's life that somehow had some meaning, although the meaning of each was still unclear. Playing a hunch, Carter went to his grandfather's medical chart and searched for his birth date. He had a general idea of how old his grandfather was, but wasn't sure if he had ever known the exact year he was born.

Searching through the details of his grandfather's admission record, he found height, weight, race, gender, and finally birth year: 1919. Applying this date against the ranges of dates on the table, it was not unreasonable that these could be stages in his grandfather's life. But what did the stages mean and why did he take such effort to outline things in this way?

With the mystery of one part of the table presumably solved, he turned to the single digits that aligned with each range of dates.

What could these mean, he wondered to himself. Were they indicators of how many children he had at some stage in his life? That didn't seem plausible because he had two daughters, yet there were three numbers on the table. Careers or jobs? That didn't seem to fit, either, as his grandfather had been an entrepreneur who was engaged in all kinds of enterprises over the course of his lifetime. He ran through possibilities around places of residence (always stayed in Tennessee), changes in faith (a lifetime Baptist), marriages (he had been married twice, not three times), and a few more wildly-conceived dead ends before finally giving up.

"You've got me stumped, Granddaddy."

He sat back in the vinyl-clad chair and looked at his

grandfather. Jack had not changed position or expression since Carter arrived yesterday. While he wasn't expecting a daily change, any difference from one day to the next would have been...well...less eerie. It was as if his grandfather had already moved on and his body, despite his advanced age and obvious declining health, just didn't know when to stop. He was like the Energizer bunny on a really slow speed.

Carter was smiling at the image when Jessica walked into the room to check Jack's vitals. She caught the tail end of Carter's smile and also noticed how it left his face when he saw her. She cocked her head at his unexpected expression.

"Hello, again, Mr. Lee," she said formally, although she felt a pang of disappointment at having to revert back to her professional demeanor.

"Hi, Jessica," Carter offered, a bit embarrassed at having been caught with a curious smile on his face, for no apparent reason. Obviously, Jack had not cracked a joke, so Carter didn't even try to explain. He didn't even know if he could.

"Did you encounter any more possums last night?" she asked, wishing for something more meaningful to say.

Carter could not help but smile, this time for real...and for a reason.

"No, no I didn't, luckily. I actually made it home without any wildlife harassing me. It was a good night." His blue eyes met hers—causing her to forget for a moment why she even came into the room.

"That's good. So I take it our little town isn't boring you too badly? Or is Atlanta already calling you home?" She took his grandfather's wrist and looked to her watch to track his pulse rate.

Her comment made Carter think about Atlanta and Mike and how, as a matter of fact, neither had called him since he had left. He was starting to wonder if Atlanta was even his home any longer.

"Quite the contrary, actually. I'm becoming quite smitten with the area. It's incredible how productive I can be without a lot of the Atlanta distractions. I can see why you stay here."

He tried to catch her eye, but her eyes remained focused on her watch, a hint of concern showing in the crinkle of her forehead and the stern gaze of her eyes.

"What? Oh, sorry. That's good. We like it here. It is a lot more livable than where I used to live."

We? Carter thought. Hopefully that's just a general 'we' and not a 'me and someone else we.' He knew she was not married, but it had not crossed his mind that she had a significant other.

"OK, well, I'll be back in later to check on Jack," she said as she turned towards the door.

"Is everything all right?" He was going to ask her where she used to live, but now Carter found himself a little concerned at what he was sensing from her about his grandfather.

Jessica hesitated in the doorway before turning to answer him.

"Yes, overall it seems so. His pulse rate has slowed from yesterday, and yesterday was a bit slower than the day before…." She looked at him and softened her voice. "We'll just watch him. It's to be expected at this point." Jessica gave him a long, consoling look, looked at his grandfather, then left to continue her rounds.

Carter let the impact of her statement sink in. He had not fully considered that his grandfather could die on his watch. This trip was only supposed to be an adventure in geriatric babysitting on his mother's behalf. His grandfather wasn't supposed to die now…with him. If he passed away this week, it would be up to Carter to break the news to his mother. He would not want some unknown healthcare worker to deliver the news in some cold, matter of fact tone, like a recitation of the daily news. No, he would definitely need to do it as this could be the hardest news his mother would ever receive.

Carter looked at the clock then, and realizing it was close to five o'clock, he began putting this day's supply of journals back in his backpack. Before he closed it up, he picked up the small binder containing the yellow legal pages, intending to put it on top. He didn't want it to get crushed by the substantially larger journals as he was still curious as to what his grandfather's table meant. Since the binder was out, he took one more look at the range of dates to see if they made any more sense. They didn't.

He was preparing to put the binder in his backpack when Jessica stuck her head in the room.

"Have you ever been to a ham supper?" she asked.

Carter looked up at her with an amused look.

"I don't think I've ever had anyone ask me that question before," he joked. "It's been a very long time since I went to a ham supper. My family and I would go to them back home, but that was a long time ago. Why?"

"The Ruritan Club up in Midway has one every couple of months and there's one tonight. It's really not a bad meal for $8. Plus, they have it by a nice river and, this time of year, you can still be outside to enjoy it. I wasn't sure if you liked to cook or eat out, so I thought I would mention it just in case you needed some options." She waited for his answer, wondering if he really knew what a ham supper was or if he was just being polite.

"Are…you…um…going to go?" he asked slowly. He had not expected an opportunity to have dinner with Jessica, but wasn't going to miss the chance. "I'm not a good crowd person if I'm alone, but it sounds like something fun to do with someone else."

She smiled despite herself.

"Yes, I was, actually. Mom and I used to do that when I'd come down to visit, so it holds some special memories for me. And the food is good. It's somewhat difficult to find, though, so I pulled one of the flyers off our break room wall. It may have directions or an address on it. I need to go home to change and run a few errands, so maybe we can meet there?"

"That sounds like a great idea. 6:00?" He was hungry, but would gladly wait to eat if he had to. He pulled a blank sheet of paper from the back of the small binder and scribbled down his cell number. The mountains were allowing him only intermittent service at best, but at least she would have his number.

"Yes, 6:00 it is. See you then, Carter." With a smile she added, "Don't get lost...OK?"

He watched her walk away and caught just a brief scent of her perfume lingering in the air before it dissipated completely. He was genuinely excited about spending time with Jessica Cooper and feeling more and more confident about the lack of any 'significant other' in her life. If there was one, he was incredibly liberal, or frequently absent, for her to be able to invite another man to dinner.

When he had flipped open the binder to get the sheet of paper, a few of the pages flipped forward and twisted against the binder ring. He didn't want them to tear, so with a gentle motion, Carter slowly folded the pages back the way they should be. As one page turned, he happened to glimpse the number '3' in very faint pencil in the upper right corner of the page. His brow furrowed.

"That's odd...," he said under his breath. He turned several more pages, looking intently now at the upper right corner of the pages until several pages over he found an even fainter '2' in the same corner.

"No way..."

He kept turning pages until at last he found a '1' on the

next page after the one he had read last night.

"Well, whaddaya know," he mumbled, feeling quite pleased about the discovery, even though it was more by accident than intellect. At least he had found the numbers and, at some later time, would figure out what they meant. For now, however, he had to go.

"Good night, Granddaddy," Carter said, touching the foot of his grandfather's bed. "I think I have a date tonight."

Midway is about a 30 minute drive from Sweet Branch on a twisty, winding, two-lane road with very little traffic. Out in rural areas, a 30 minute trip for dinner may seem ludicrous. But when you live in a large city with 5 million other people, 30 minutes is just a trip to the grocery store that's only 5 miles away. I didn't mind the short drive at all, and I was more than ready for a break from my little two-day routine. It didn't hurt that I would be spending it with Jessica.

When I was young, my parents and I would go to this very ham supper most every time it was offered. The Midway Ruritan Club has a little red building set off from the main road that lies along Asbury Creek. In summer, the doors of the Ruritan building swing wide open allowing the breeze to flow through and the feeding line of hungry customers to meander in whatever formation it wants. Most everyone eats outside in the warmer weather because the surrounding area is just too picturesque to ignore. In fall and winter, the ham supper becomes a more intimate affair as everyone, Ruritaner and customer alike, crowds inside the confines of the little red building. On nights when every family-style table is filled to capacity and the line of hungry diners winds out the door, the din of conversation and laughter competes with the slapping of utensils on plates for the most attention. It's deafening and tantalizing all at the same time.

The 750i hugged the corners of the two-lane road that took me to where the Ruritan Club building sat near Asbury Creek. Small road signs named for past landowners greeted me every quarter or half mile. Lester Snapp Road. Bud Ball Road. Lola Humphreys Road. Some who never sought fame now have their names permanently affixed to a green reflective sign atop an eight foot shaft of steel, a legacy for people who time would otherwise forget. No one dares change the signs that have marked their path home for so many years…it's too much trouble and they'd never get the new road names right when giving directions to some unsuspecting soul lost in the country on a harmless Sunday drive.

Up ahead I see the familiar scene of the river, the Ruritan building, and the rows of cars in the makeshift parking lot created just for the ham supper. It occurs to me that I have no idea what type of car Jessica drives, what she's wearing, or where she plans to meet me. I take a minute to scan the area, but see no one resembling Jessica in any way. I do, however, see lots of orange…orange coats, hats, visors, and what isn't orange is emblazoned with a large orange 'T'…the logo of the Tennessee Volunteers. Unless Jessica is a die-hard Vol fan, it should be relatively easy to find her in this environment—she'll be the only one, besides me, without some patch of orange on her person.

Pulling into a spot on the end, partially due to convenience, but also due to the shameful protectiveness I laud over my car, I roll up the windows and kill the engine. I happen to glance in the rear-view mirror and see Jessica walking towards me. Her hair is not in a pony-tail this time, but instead flows over a gray sweatshirt accented by a pair of faded blue jeans. In her hand is a cell phone and what appears to be the sheet on which I had written my cell phone number. She meets me at the door as I climb out.

"Well, you made it after all!" she said with somewhat of an incredulous look on her face.

I offered back a look of surprise.

"Why do you say that? You didn't think I'd come? It's a ham supper—how does one pass that up?" I joked. Of course, I'm here more for the company than the dinner...

"It's not that, I just didn't think you could find the place. This place is off the beaten path, and if you're not familiar with the area, you can easily end up in another county."

"Oh, no. I can read directions and I left in plenty of time to get here. I would even have stopped and asked for help if these directions weren't working for me."

She cocked her head quizzically.

"What directions?"

"Uh....from the flyer?" more of a question than a response. Up until now, I had not thought about it, but it was apparently becoming a serious situation.

"REALLY now. Can I see them?"

"Sure..." I pulled her flyer from my pocket and opened it up to read the flyer aloud.

"The Midway Ruritan Club will have a ham supper on Wednesday, October 17, from 4:30-7:30 P.M. at the Midway Ruritan Club Building in Asbury Creek Park. The price is $8 per person. The menu will include fried country ham, vegetables, salad, biscuits and gravy, dessert, and beverage. Carry-out will be available."

I felt a tinge of red wash over my face as I realized the flyer did NOT have directions and yet I had so confidently credited it for getting me here...to a little building...way out in the middle of Timbuktu, Tennessee. Uh, oh.

"Well, huh...would you look at that." I looked up at her sheepishly and tried my best coy smile.

"Yes, what about that?" She was not angry, but definitely curious about how in the world I had pulled this off. "That's why I was going to call you. I didn't realize the flyer lacked directions until just a few minutes ago. I was afraid you were sitting lost somewhere or were just going to give up and—" she stopped before finishing the thought. "I don't think the Midway Ruritan building is a point of interest in most onboard GPS systems," she said as she pointed at my car, "You'll have to enlighten me on your amazing directional ability."

I thought about it for a moment. "I think I can do that. It may take a while, though," I replied with a grin.

Jessica smiled in return. "We at least have dinner to discuss it…" she said, letting her words trail off.

As we began walking towards the freshly-painted Ruritan building, she turned back for a moment to look at my car.

"I love the color of your car, by the way, and you just can't go wrong with a leather interior."

"Yes, leather wears well and I'm a sucker for the barbera red." I was trying not to sound patronizing, even though there was more to such a piece of machinery than just a pretty paint job. "The leather is a little hot in the Atlanta summer, but aside from that, it's worth the money."

Jessica turned and began walking toward the building again. "I'm curious…did you get the sport suspension option? I know it's not standard on the 750i, but if you're going to invest in a power plant like that, you at least need the right suspension to get the most out of it. The extra money is worth it, I think, considering you have 360 horses in that beauty." The ends of her mouth began curling up in that captivating little grin again.

Her question was not one I was expecting, and I was surprised and impressed at the same time.

"As a matter of fact I did get the sport suspension," I said slowly. "Wow, how in the world did you know about that?"

"Oh, let's say I've had friends with cars like that and I get an earful about how wonderful they are. Besides, I love the way they look. You probably don't get much of a chance to wind it up, so to speak, in Atlanta." The sparkle in her eye made me wonder if she was talking about the car or something entirely different. I searched her face for any clue before I continued, but she offered none.

"No, there aren't a lot of opportunities to run full throttle on twisting roads where I live. But from time-to-time, like getting here, I can put it through its paces." I leaned closer. "I think I'm not the only person with some interesting things to share tonight..."

Jessica just laughed as we headed into the building and the waiting throng of diners.

A brief stay in a long line of hungry Tennesseans resulted in two plates covered with fried country ham, biscuits, gravy, fried okra, cole slaw and more, just as the flyer had promised. Carter and Jessica slowly wound their way through the maze of tables, and their wide-bodied occupants, until they found a private corner at the end of a long picnic table.

Carter had not realized how hungry he really was until the scent of frying ham and home-baked goods teased him in the serving line. Jessica, equally famished, suddenly felt a little self-conscious at the amount of food on her plate, although in the back of her mind she was already prioritizing the dessert selection on the other side of the room. As Jessica unfolded her white paper napkin across her lap, she avoided eye contact with Carter so she wouldn't get too flustered so early in the evening. Carter caught himself staring at her and quickly looked away before she noticed. They began eating, one stealing occasional glances at the other, until Jessica broke the silence between them.

"OK, Carter. Now, tell me how you found this place so easily." There were many other questions in her mind, such as his reluctance to divulge his true vocation, or why a corporate executive would be compelled to sit with a dying man when he could have easily paid a sitter to do it. But an answer to this simple question would be a good starting point.

"Truth is, I'm from this area," he sheepishly admitted. "Grew up in Johnson City, just down the road, and lived there until I left for college. My parents and I used to come down here to this very ham supper quite a bit. I could find this place blindfolded. When you made the suggestion, it brought back a lot of memories for me as well."

"So why didn't you tell me you were from here?" Are you ashamed of it, she wondered?

He shrugged. "You didn't ask, and quite frankly, I didn't think it was important. I guess I've seen people try to leverage where they are from, who they know, or some inconsequential fact they think will either impress you or persuade you to do something for them. I didn't want you to think I was trying to do any of that."

Fair enough, she thought. She hadn't considered that and, to be honest, he had not tried to mislead her. He just didn't go into tremendous detail.

"My turn now," he said. "Where do you call home? Where do your folks live?"

"My father died when I was a teenager, then my mother passed away about five years ago. She lived in Sweet Branch, but that's not where I grew up. I'm from a little town in North Carolina called Goldsboro."

"Oh, I'm sorry. I didn't know."

"What? Is it bad to be from Goldsboro?"

"No, I mean your parents. I didn't know they had passed."

"That's OK, I didn't expect you to know that...but

thanks. I miss them both a lot, though. Especially my mom. She was my best friend because for many years it was just the two of us. Even now, I find myself wanting to pick up the phone and call her or go see her. But I can't..." Her voice trailed off, but only for a second before she regained her composure.

Jessica continued. "She's the reason I'm here now. When she was diagnosed with terminal cancer, I left my job in D.C. and moved down here to take care of her. Been down here ever since."

"You were a nurse in D.C.?"

"No..." Now it was her turn to share. "I was a private equity consultant. I was part of a boutique firm that handled all the typical merger and acquisition fare for the well-heeled in the greater Washington area."

Carter could feel the uncontrollable look of surprise flash across his face.

"You worked in M&A?"

His reaction made her uncomfortable.

"Yes, I did." She gave him her best negotiating glare. "Does that surprise you for some reason?" she asked pointedly.

"Um....yes, a little, but only because I've seen you taking care of my grandfather and you just seemed so natural at it. I can't imagine you tearing some poor schmuck a new one as he presented his best offer."

His complement flattered and warmed her, both for its praise and for its confirmation that he had noticed more about her than just the care she provided his grandfather.

"I was not a lead negotiator. Not my cup of tea. I was more of an advisor on structuring capital for private equity deals. Rich people like to sell their toys to each other and, somehow, everyone seems to make money in the process. Not a bad business."

She was piquing his curiosity now.

"So why did you leave it?" By now she was increasingly more interesting than the remains of his ham plate. He had stopped eating and was focused completely on her next words. Carter couldn't fathom how someone who knew the ins and outs of the deal world would ever leave it. Unimaginable.

Jessica thought for a moment because, up until now, no one had ever asked. She had never articulated a complete reason to anyone for why she started her life over.

"It's complicated, but the simple answer is it didn't feel like me any longer. I had worked so hard to get where I was and one day something happened that just made me feel like it was all for naught. It was not a good feeling. It was the same time that Mom's cancer was diagnosed as terminal, so I moved down here to take care of her. I'm an only child, so I was all she had. After she died, the idea of being back in the deal game again didn't feel right to me. Something had to change. I realized I felt very comfortable taking care of Mom, so I decided to turn it into a new career. It was a big accomplishment for me to make that decision and take a new road, after everything I had invested in my business career."

"Do you ever regret it?" he asked thoughtfully. He could not conceive of a life without a business deal or some type of project lurking just over the horizon. What does one do, he wondered.

Jessica thought about it for a moment, wanting to be completely honest.

"No, I really don't. I think about it from time-to-time, and I DID enjoy it for the most part. But I can't say I miss it. I think where I'm going is better than where I've been, and I don't think I'll ever regret leaving."

Carter thought about the things happening at work and the effect defining moments like that have on a person. He was nowhere near leaving his job to go off and do something completely different, but it was reassuring to know that someone in what he considered a prestigious and challenging profession had hit a bump in the road, as well, and survived.

"Good for you. Recently I've actually had a few thoughts about a change myself."

"Like what?" she asked.

"Well...I...uh...I guess I haven't thought about it in that much detail yet. But a change could have some merit." He was nervously swirling the remains of his sweet tea until it about sloshed out of the cup.

"What did you say you did for a living? An accountant?" Jessica posed the question to see whether he would be forthcoming about what he did.

This wasn't a question he really wanted to answer. Carter wasn't sure how she would perceive him being a corporate executive, or whether it would make any difference at all. He was sensitive to anything that would make her feel uncomfortable or confused.

"Well...not exactly. My official title is Sr. Vice President of Global Development and Acquisitions. I work for Associated Media Limited. We have a large presence in the media business. Print, television, radio, and the like. The simple description of my job is that I look for companies and operations to buy and, if everything works out, we make the buy happen. It's really an all-consuming job."

"I see. So tell me, Carter...why did you do the deal with Acuity Broadcasting?"

He stared at her for a moment.

"Wha...what?" He could not hide his reaction and threw up his hands in amazement. "How do you know anything about that?" Carter was seeing an entirely different side of Jessica Cooper. She was coming at him from all angles and it was keeping him honest. And it made her more attractive than ever to him.

"Your name sounded familiar to me but I couldn't place it. I was curious so I Googled you last night and low and behold, there you were being quoted about the merits of the deal." Jessica smiled. She continued with her explanation.

"Being in equity consulting, I still have an interest in money and markets. I trade my own portfolio, and I had entered a position with Associated to play the earnings momentum. Everything had just settled when your announcement came out about the whole buyout of Acuity. When the market didn't like your offer and your stock tanked, it took me underwater as well. It was dead money for quite awhile and, in retrospect, I should have cut my losses and bailed. So since that deal caused me some grief, and I have you as a captive audience, I thought I'd ask." Nicely done, she thought.

Carter picked up his cup and took his time finishing off the last of the tea, and a few ice cubes for good measure.

"I'd like to cloak myself under a confidentiality obligation, but since the deal has been closed for awhile, I guess that won't work," he said jokingly. By now, Carter had given up any pretense of trying to keep both his history and his career private. This woman was somehow able to leave him bare and exposed, with little to no effort, in the time required to consume a fried ham dinner. And most important to him—she had been curious enough about him to check him out on Google.

"To answer your question, Acuity had a hodge-podge of radio station programming formats in its portfolio, and none of them were working in their particular markets. They were playing easy listening in a predominately minority area and the hip-hop stations were wiping them out. Then you had a pre-1990s country format, what you could call 'twangy' country, in one of the mid-sized cities that liked rock-a-billy country. The problems went on and on. So, we did two things: we restructured their debt into longer-term instruments to help with cash flow and then, we reformatted just about every station to focus on the Hispanic market. The stations that didn't fit the Hispanic demographic were sold off. I think you would agree that the market eventually rewarded us for that."

It was true. After about six months, Associated Media was trading near an all-time high for the period. And she had made out all right on the deal.

"You know you got lucky with that ... right?"

"You think? How so?" He gave her a questioning gaze.

"Because Acuity had been hemorrhaging cash for a long time. They couldn't get an ounce worth of revenue growth and honestly, you really haven't, either. What you did do, however, was make a poorly managed organization operate efficiently. But your reformatting strategy really didn't buy you anything, and after the upcoming election revenue blip, my guess is that you'll sell the whole package."

Carter watched her eyes as she spoke and he saw the fire that smoldered below the surface. He engaged her gaze and held it, focusing first on the right eye, then the left eye, before settling back on her right eye...the intimate eye.

"Jessica Cooper, I have to say I have never met anyone like you before." He wanted to take her hand, but decided against it. It was too early. "But I'm very glad I have now."

She felt his stare and thought to herself, I'm glad you have, too. Her gaze at this point was slowly drifting from friendly to wistful...almost longing. She felt a connection to him and the more time they spent together, the stronger she felt it.

"You know...I didn't get the feeling you liked me very much the first time we met," he said as casually as he could. "So it was a nice surprise when you invited me to dinner." He watched her face for her reaction.

"I wouldn't say that," she said. "I guess I'm just protective of my patients. I tend to be extra suspicious of people who say they are family 'coming to help' as they often have other intentions...like getting signatures on wills."

Carter placed his napkin and used silverware on his plate. "Personally, I think it's wonderful that you're that way. Some of us haven't a clue about what we're doing when it comes to taking care of older people." He smiled. "I'm glad he's in your hands."

Before she could respond, he continued.

"So...can I get a second shot at this whole first impression thing?"

Jessica smiled briefly before lowering her gaze.

"Hmmmm. I guess anyone who would sacrifice a BMW for the life of a little possum can't be all bad....so...yes." She looked up at him, her fork stopping in midair. "Besides...you were really funny trying to figure out if I was married." She gave him an 'I caught you' look before taking another bite.

Carter raised his eyebrows.

"Really? Funny? I thought I was being rather coy about it all." He looked around, slightly embarrassed.

Jessica laughed. "No...not so much, Carter." Her voice softened. "But I was glad you asked."

He let her words sink in for a moment before responding.

"I am, too, Jessica. And I'm really glad you invited me out tonight. I —" He stopped, surprised at the openness he felt toward her. Carter didn't want to make her uncomfortable by saying too much the first time they were alone together. But the look in her eyes told him it was OK, that she wanted to know. So he continued.

"I just wanted a chance to talk...outside of the hospice center. Thank you for making tonight happen."

The warmth of his eyes made her want to crawl across the table and into his arms. The intense feelings made no sense to her, but she felt them every time he smiled or looked at her now. Walking in together from the parking lot, she could smell his cologne and wondered what it would be like to be closer to his face, kissing his neck…tasting his lips. She caught herself and scrambled for a more benign thought.

"You're welcome, Carter. It sounds like we both wanted to be here…I'm glad you wanted to come."

Carter studied her face, warmed by their exchange. He felt deeply thankful to the Midway Ruritan Club for having their ham supper tonight, otherwise they would have not had the excuse to spend the evening together. He was contemplating making an extra donation to whatever causes they supported when he noticed the dining room was almost empty. The ham supper was not a late affair and some of the older Ruritans were glancing over their way to see how much longer they may be. $8 bought them a full plate of food, but it didn't reserve the building for the night.

"It appears that everyone is starting to pack up for the night. I have a few beers in the fridge at my grandfather's house if you'd like to come over and talk for a little while…" With a slight smile he added, "It's still early…and I don't want the night to end yet."

She understood completely what he meant. Even though they had only known each other for a short time, they already had a very comfortable togetherness.

"I would love to. Can I follow you? I don't know where you're staying, nor do I know all these back roads as well as you natives do," she said with a wink.

"Of course you can. I'll even keep my 360 horses under control and not leave you in the dust. And if you're lucky, I may even introduce you to the canine friend I've met…if she's hanging around tonight, that is. She's a sweet one."

As they stood to leave, Jessica gently placed her hand on Carter's back.

"Lead the way, Mr. Lee."

On the drive back to the farmhouse, Carter kept a close eye on the lights behind him. Even though she had been in the area awhile, back roads can be confusing enough in daylight, much less the dark of an autumn night. He certainly didn't want to lose her; he wanted to spend a little more time with her.

Jessica had presented an entirely new side of herself tonight, validating his initial feelings that she was somehow different. Special. Her attractiveness notwithstanding, he found himself drawn to the way she honed in on what she wanted to know and directly asked for it. And at least on the question about the Acuity deal, she was very well-versed in business. He hadn't thought about selling the Acuity properties after this year's elections, but it wasn't a bad idea. Assuming he still had a job when he returned to Atlanta, he might have one of his analysts look into the possibility.

Thirty minutes later, he pulled into his grandfather's gravel driveway and Jessica pulled in directly beside him. Carter had forgotten to leave any outside lights on, so the only illumination on the graveled, uneven ground was the yellow light of the harvest moon. He met Jessica as she exited her truck and offered an arm for support.

"The sidewalk is in pathetic shape, unfortunately," he explained, "and I would feel terrible if I let you fall on your first visit here. Can I escort you?"

"Of course," she laughed. "I didn't know men from the big city could be so considerate." She slipped her hand through the crook of his arm and gave it a gentle squeeze.

He smiled in the darkness.

"I think if you grow up in the South, it's ingrained in you from birth."

"I'm certainly not complaining."

He moved carefully down the slope of the driveway and

maneuvered over the deteriorating walk before reaching the front porch. Though he needed his hand to reach his keys, he was very careful not to release her hand from his arm. He pulled his arm tighter against his side as if to reinforce the point. Key obtained, he unlatched the door and led her into the house.

She waited as he switched on the lights. Immediately upon entering the house, she sensed the concentration of stale, musty air that had hit Carter on his first night. As the lights came up, Jessica took in the room and its contents, and then cast a look towards Carter.

"Quaint. A lot of pretty antiques."

"That's one way to describe it, I guess. It seems like a place that's frozen in time. When I first arrived, the smell was a bit overwhelming. It's become a lot more tolerable now, however."

No, Carter, I think your sense of smell just gave up, Jessica thought to herself.

"Has this house been in your family for awhile?"

Carter moved to the kitchen and grabbed two of the remaining beers from the refrigerator before responding.

"It has. My great-grandparents built the house around the turn of the century and it has stayed in the family ever since. I think my family has tried to make it modern over the years and, for the most part, they've succeeded. It has all the basic necessities." He put the bottles on the table and rooted around in one of the kitchen drawers for the bottle opener. "I know I just had that out just yesterday. Where did I put it?"

Jessica slowly walked around the room while Carter was in the kitchen. She was getting an opportunity to see the other side of one of her patient's lives—their real life. Usually all she had to go on with a new resident was whatever their children or guardian told her, and whatever the patient was able to relay themselves. With Jack Bailey, however, she was able to see where he lived, what he used, and what he cherished. It was a very special opportunity and she didn't want to miss a thing.

"Sorry that took so long. I couldn't find the bottle opener and these don't twist off." Carter noticed her serious expression and intense gaze at the pictures on the wall. "Is everything all right?" he asked as he handed her a beer.

"Yes, absolutely. Sorry, I was just admiring the pictures on the wall. Do you know who they are?"

Carter took a swig of the beer.

"The one in the middle is my grandfather's mother...my great-grandmother, rather," he explained as he motioned towards a deep walnut frame containing the fixed gaze of a round faced, dark-haired woman. "She built the house along with my great-grandfather. He's the one on the left."

"I see. Who is the gentleman on the right?"

Carter looked hard at the picture. It was not as dark or sepia toned as the other pictures, but looked old nonetheless. The man in the photograph was looking off to the right and appeared to have been recorded for posterity speaking in mid-sentence.

"I don't believe I know. It may have been a cousin or a brother or someone once removed from either my great-grandparents or my grandfather." He took another drink of the beer. "Sometimes all these folks just look the same to me, and once my grandfather passes, we may never know who they are." The truth of his words had not occurred to him until that moment.

He looked at her.

"That's sad, isn't it?"

Jessica nodded her agreement.

"So much history is lost when an older person passes. They've seen and experienced so much. Unless somehow they find a way to share it, it dies with them."

They moved over to the table that housed all of Jack Bailey's journals.

"What are all these—" She caught herself mid-sentence. "I'm sorry, Carter. I don't mean to be so nosy. This is just such a rare thing for me...to find out the personal side of someone I'm taking care of. It just makes Jack real to me." She touched his arm for emphasis.

He nodded, swiftly, almost awkwardly.

"No, I don't think you're nosy at all." He caught her gaze as he spoke. "It's nice, actually, to know you care that much. He seemed like a really great guy."

"Seemed?" Jessica repeated. "He's still here, Carter," she reminded him softly.

He felt a pang of guilt at dismissing his grandfather's life before he was gone.

"You're right. Bad choice of words. I'm just feeling like the end is inevitable at this point."

She couldn't argue with his reasoning, and was a bit embarrassed at how overt she had become in inquiring about Jack Bailey's personal effects. She changed the subject away from the books on the table.

"You must have been very close to him to be here like this, considering how many obligations you must already have...with your job and all." Jessica put her beer on the table just long enough to take off her jacket and lay it over the chair near the front door. She moved to the sofa, sat down, and curled up against the back, resting her head against the crocheted afghan lying on top.

Carter turned and joined her on the couch, noticing how comfortable and natural it seemed for them to be talking this way. He chose his words carefully before he spoke.

"I didn't know him like everyone else did. In fact, I really didn't know him at all. I wanted to, though. I think a lot of men view their grandfathers as the ideal man—wise, thoughtful, fun, and caring. Grandfathers are supposed to be those patient sages who embody the best of what a man is supposed to be."

He felt her gaze, but heard nothing from her.

"I was the youngest grandchild. It seemed that whenever we had reunions, my cousins received most of the attention. They were louder, stronger, more demanding. I was left out. He knew my name, I knew he was my grandfather, but that was about it. We never really progressed from there. My dad's father died when I was very young, so I only had one chance to have any type of grandfather/grandson relationship. It didn't happen."

"How did that make you feel?" she asked, wanting to understand. She was recalling her own memories of being an only child and how easy it could be to feel completely isolated in your own family.

Carter leaned back, feeling his arm come to rest on her knees that were pulled up onto the sofa. She didn't protest.

"I...felt..." he said as he turned to her, "sad...as if I had missed out on something I was supposed to have..." He fidgeted with the label on his beer. "Something that I needed."

He thought some more.

"And I guess I still feel that way..." Carter searched her face for her reaction.

"I understand," she offered. "My grandmother grew up here, but moved to Indiana when she married my grandfather. Mom and Dad were married there, but moved to North Carolina, so I only saw my grandparents once or twice a year. They were older and couldn't travel very well and Dad's job didn't give us enough time off to make that long journey any more frequently than we did. Plus, I think he hated the drive."

She took a drink and continued.

"So, I know what you mean about missing out. I enjoyed visiting with my grandparents, but that was really all we did: visited. There was no chance to spend the time together that you need to build a relationship, to let them know about all the day-to-day things that go on in your life...the little things that can define who you are. I was very close with my mother and I like to think that my grandmother was just like her. But I just don't know for certain...and I hate that."

Jessica had a way of making Carter feel like anything he thought or shared was important. It was uncommon for him to venture into his personal thoughts and feelings, but he was drawn to the complete acceptance she offered.

He hesitated a moment, wanting to give her a chance to finish her thoughts.

"Do you ever wonder about the lives your grandparents lived?"

Jessica moved to face him more directly.

"What do you mean?"

Carter mirrored her position with his own.

"You know, the day-to-day stuff like you mentioned: what they did, what they worried about, what they thought their purpose was. All the stuff that we do, only 50, 60, 70 years earlier. Do you ever wonder about their lives...who they were and what they were like...pre-you?"

"You mean like genealogy and family trees? That kind of stuff?"

Carter got up from the sofa and walked over to the desk on which his grandfather's journals rested. He chose an older, more worn journal to illustrate his point and carried it back to the antique sofa.

"No, the very essence of their existence...the minutia of their lives...day-by-day." He put the journal in Jessica's hands and motioned for her to open it.

She placed her empty bottle on the table in front of her and wiped the moisture from her fingers onto her jeans. The cover of the book was worn, but still carried the rich smell of leather tanned eons ago. Turning the cover, she was greeted by yellowing pages filled with an unfamiliar, but very legible, handwriting. Jessica began reading the first few sentences to herself until she realized what she had in her hands.

"Your grandfather kept journals?"

Carter nodded slowly.

"How many?"

He glanced toward the table, her eyes following his.

"You mean all those?"

"Yep. I think there is one there for every year of his life from age twenty until last year."

"But why?"

Jessica was honestly amazed. Coupled with her natural curiosity about those dying faces for which she cared, the presence of a living history cemented her intrigue.

Carter shrugged and shook his head.

"I wish I knew. I stumbled on them purely by accident when I was looking for something to keep me occupied at the center. By themselves, they are interesting enough, but there is something else."

He went to get his backpack to show her the binder he had discovered. The excitement he felt was not unlike a child showing his parent a spelling test with a yellow smiley face from the teacher.

"I found this sitting on top, like it had been placed there to be found." He put the binder in her hands.

Jessica studied it before opening it and turning the first few pages.

"What is this?" she asked.

"I wondered that myself when I first found it. I'm still not convinced I've figured it out, but from what I can tell, he wrote a synopsis of his life. Things he remembered and things that stood out when he looked back over his years. I haven't read beyond the first narrative yet, but I think this binder is the result of his efforts." He paused, allowing her time to flip through the pages. "A few things had me confused, however. May I?" He held out his hand.

"By all means. I'm intrigued," she said as she handed him the binder.

Carter took it and turned to the first page of writing.

"The last paragraph of the first narrative just stops." He pointed to the paragraph and read the last sentence to its curious conclusion. "I skimmed the beginning of the second narrative, but it went down a completely different path. So the first mystery is why he just stopped mid-sentence before explaining what he wanted someone to know."

Jessica was as curious as Carter about what his grandfather meant to say, but she thought she may know why the sentence just ended on a partial thought.

"Sometimes older people lose their train of thought and can't recover it. It's not uncommon. And considering all that he has written just in this binder," she said, flipping quickly through the pages, "he had a good run before his focus went off track."

"That's a good point," Carter conceded. "I hadn't considered that. If that's the case, chances are he didn't notice it and doesn't answer the question anywhere else. Which means I may never figure it out." The potential of that reality was disappointing to Carter.

Jessica touched his hand.

"Don't assume that. He could surprise you and provide a full explanation in some other place. I'm surprised you didn't read deeper into the narrative today."

He looked at her and smiled.

"I was going to, but I had something more interesting come up this evening." Jessica felt herself blush.

He continued. "While he wasn't able to finish that sentence, he was able to include this rather curious table on the same page." Carter tapped it with his finger for emphasis. "Mystery number two..."

She studied it for a minute.

"Interesting...no clue what it means?"

"Not exactly," he paused, then smiled. "But I have a theory. See if this makes sense. The dates seem to identify certain portions of his life. He was born in 1919 and the first journal was written about the time he was 20."

She looked at the table and doing the quick math in her head, concurred.

"OK. He would have been 20 in 1939. Go on."

"It appears he divided his life into sections from that point forward. I inferred that from these numbers to the right of the sections." He pointed at the single digits that followed each range of dates. "But I'm not sure what differentiated one section of his life from another. I thought I had another dead end on my hands until..."

He flipped the yellow page forward and pulled the corner to her. She was pressing against his shoulder now, absorbed into his energy and the intrigue of what he had found.

"See?"

She squinted at the paper. After a second, she noticed the pale pencil tracing of the number '1.'

Jessica looked at Carter.

"Whoa, I would have missed that completely."

Carter nodded. "I nearly missed it, too. It was sheer luck that I even noticed it. But I think that's what the numbers mean because I found a '2' and a '3' farther back in the binder. My grandfather must have intended for the journals to be read in sections, followed by the appropriate synopsis from the binder of that period in his life." He looked at the page and then to her for her reaction.

A tiny smile started in the corner of her mouth, but quickly disappeared. He suddenly felt a bit defensive about her seeming to laugh at what he had shared. Jessica sensed the change immediately and responded as if reading his mind.

"I'm not laughing, Carter. This is just incredibly interest-ing—I think I have chills. I feel like we're in a Nancy Drew mystery." The honesty of her statement reflected in her eyes and extinguished any concern Carter had about continuing.

He smiled.

"I haven't heard that name in awhile. Should I refer to you as Nancy from now on?"

Jessica, tickled at the notion of poking around Jack Bai-ley's old farmhouse to find hidden journals and maybe even treasure maps, couldn't stifle her giggle.

"I'll tell you what. I'll be Nancy Drew if you'll be one of the Hardy Boys."

"OK, you can do that...if you can tell me either one of their names," he said with a boyish grin.

Both of them burst into laughter at the realization that neither could remember the name of either Hardy brother.

Jessica moved in closer.

"I guess you dodged that one, didn't you?" she teased. "I'll just have to call you 'Hardy Boy' from here on...just because."

Carter liked making her laugh...he loved it, actually. He knew he had been talking about something somewhat important before, but right now, he didn't remember—nor care.

"So what are you going to do?" she asked.

"About...?"

"About the journals, silly. Are you going to read them all?" Now he remembered.

"Oh. Yes. In fact, I've already started. And as silly as it sounds, I'm going to follow the table, too, and see if my hunch is right. He did this for a reason...I guess I want to know what that reason is."

She read his face as he spoke, inferring what he didn't say.

"The journals mean a lot to you, don't they...."

He stared ahead for a moment, unconsciously tightening his grip on the journal he held.

"They do. I always wanted to know him, and I feel this is the last chance I'll have." He looked down at the floor. "I feel guilty about our relationship, too."

His statement caught her off guard. She waited for him to continue.

"When I was young, I used to think he should have tried to get to know me...to give us a relationship," Carter said, a tinge of bitterness in his voice. "I think I was angry with him for years, but never really knew it." He paused.

"But in recent years, I haven't done anything to get to know him...and I should have. I could easily have called, written, or even come to visit, but I didn't. I didn't treat him any better than how I believed he treated me. I just never realized it until now."

He took her hand and turned his face toward hers.

"I feel guilty being the one he may have to die with."

"Carter, I am with people every day who would give anything to die with someone by their side," she offered. Her memory of the night her mother died flashed into her mind and she felt the emotions as clearly as if her mother had just passed. She acknowledged his feelings, and hers, by gently squeezing his hand.

Carter continued. "I had a dream the other night about him. It was so very real. It was like he was right here and knew I was here. I dreamt he was trying to tell me something. Do you think that's crazy?"

"No, I don't," she confided. "I felt my mother's presence close by even after she passed. It was so real that it limited my ability to accept the finality of it all. Some nights, when we know a patient is close to death and has no family or friends nearby, I stay with them just so they don't have to be alone. Sometimes they know I'm there, sometimes they don't. But I always know."

Her words touched his heart, making him wonder what it would feel like to be loved by this woman whose heart and compassion must have no bounds. Through her words and touch he was beginning to realize the limitations of his own person and how much he may have been missing in his life, and how much others may have missed from him.

"There's a lot I don't understand about things, Carter, but some things we don't have to understand…we just have to believe."

Her dark eyes spoke to him beyond what mere words could convey, and for a second he felt as if a part of him had finally found its equal. Carter longed to kiss her, but hesitated past the moment.

The clock on the mantle suddenly announced the arrival of the eleventh hour, startling both of them from their pending intimacy. Jessica looked to her watch for confirmation.

"I don't know where the time went," she sighed. "I guess I should be going. Morning comes early for me." She lingered out of longing before releasing her hand from Carter's. Her face could not hide her disappointment.

"Yeah, I guess you do have an early morning," Carter conceded, feeling the remorse of letting the moment pass. "I'll walk you out."

He helped her with her jacket and threw on an old barn jacket hanging next to the door to ward off the chill of the October night. Carter turned on the porch lamp, but even with the benefit of additional light, she still held his arm on their walk back across the uneven sidewalk. This time, however, it was more out of want than need. They remained intertwined until they reached Jessica's truck, neither willing to be the one to first release their grasp.

Carter took a deep breath.

"Thanks for inviting me to the dinner tonight. I really

enjoyed…everything…" He let his words trail off. They were like comfortable friends now. Beyond the point of mere acquaintances, but not yet touching the space where he felt he could draw her in like he longed to do. They allowed silence to fill the space between them, lingering, then he felt her arms go around his neck and the curves of her body close to his own. He circled her waist with his arms and buried his face in her hair, pulling her close to him. They stood together for several minutes, gently swaying as those feeling the rush of new love tend to do. There was so much he felt but was unable to put into words, so he remained silent.

"Good night, Carter," she whispered, then placed a gentle kiss on his cheek as she pulled away. She climbed into her truck and rolled down the window before she began to pull away.

"Would you like to come over for dinner tomorrow night? I may not be able to beat the Midway ham supper, but I'll give it my best try."

"I would love it…we'll make plans tomorrow…" Carter smiled, almost laughing at how little convincing it would take for him to be anywhere with Jessica.

She smiled in the darkness. "It's a date then. Good night, Carter…"

He touched her arm through the open window.

"Good night, Jessica. And…"

She waited for him to finish.

"Watch out for possums."

She laughed in response, then rolled up the window. He watched her back out of the long driveway and waited until her taillights disappeared over the hill before heading back into the house.

Carter took off his barn jacket and made the rounds turning off the lights before he turned in for the night. As he looked around the room one last time, his eye caught the clock sitting on the mantle that just moments earlier had signaled the end of their evening together. The old Regulator clock sat perfectly still, sitting dead on 11:00 p.m., its pendulum as still as it had been since he arrived. He remembered its rhythmic tick-tock from years ago, when as a young boy he played in his grandparents' living room. But he couldn't recall if it had been working since he arrived, or if he had simply ignored it. Carter had not wound it since he had been staying here and, until it had chimed earlier in the evening, he had not paid it any mind. He gave it one more look, then headed up to the bedroom for the night.

Midnight found me still staring at the ceiling, wide awake, and nowhere near drowsy. For the past hour or so I had relived the events of the evening with Jessica, how our relationship had moved from two individuals sharing a meal to two people sharing intimate thoughts, feelings, and fears. I could still smell the faint scent of her perfume on my shirt, keeping her very much a part of my thoughts. I could spend the rest of the night with her at the forefront of my mind, but I knew that would only keep me awake. THAT I did not want, so I decided to read on into my grandfather's next narrative in the hope of drifting off for the night.

I padded down the narrow hallway to the creaking wooden steps that lead to the living room. The logistics of maneuvering around the aging farmhouse had become second nature to me in just a few days, so I required no light to find my way. The backpack was just where I had left it, and after feeling around the edges for the zipper, I opened it to find the small binder sitting right on top. Careful not to inadvertently pull any pages away, I lifted it out and made my way back to the bedroom.

At my condo in Atlanta, I had installed two halogen spotlights just above my headboard to allow me adequate light to lie in bed and work or read. My grandfather's house, however, had some sixty watt lights scattered here and there, but nothing more than a forty watt bulb in the small lamp beside the brass bed. Considering the light penciling of his writings against the yellow paper, it would be an exercise in focusing to extract each and every word. But maybe that will help bring on sleep, I thought. I flipped the pages to the narrative he had denoted as '1' and began to read.

Many years ago, I met a woman and fell in love. I had longed for what I considered the perfect woman: beautiful, gracious, kind, and loving, and in Emma, I felt I had found her. We married and began a life together with little more than the few possessions we had between us and our shared hopes and aspirations. To supplement the farm, I started a small business that I was committed to seeing succeed because, with that success, I could take care of my family in the way I felt I should. I gave a tremendous amount of myself to my business, and it was not long before it began to thrive and prosper. With each successful year came new opportunities and I devoted more and more time to these ventures. Life was good, and I knew this would make my wife incredibly happy…because it was for us.

Or so I thought.

One afternoon I arrived home early from a business trip and found the house strangely quiet. There are times when you sense something is not right, and this was one of those times. I began to notice that a few things were missing. Not significant items, but ones that I knew my wife held dear and I was concerned that a horrible theft of her prized possessions had occurred. Then I saw the envelope.

On the table in the kitchen sat a simple white envelope with my name on the outside. I picked it up and inside, on my wife's bonded stationary, was a letter, written in her distinct handwriting, addressed to me. It read:

Dear Jack,

I realized today I finally have to confront what I did not want to acknowledge. This gift of us that had once held such splendor has transformed into a meaningless nightmare for me. I would give all that I am to return to a place where time existed only for our happiness and pleasure, but it's impossible. One thing became very clear to me today: I have to leave you.

There is nothing more I can give and nothing more I can do. My feelings of us left long ago. I realize I have been losing the very person I am, little by little, for several months. I was content to let the world revolve around your wishes and desires, but that's not how it is supposed to be. I can no longer take the nights of exasperation, of lying alone…regardless of whether you are next to me or away. I wanted everything for you; gave what little I had to sustain your wants, needs, and desires. If only you had done the same for me. I toiled and sweated to make our house a home, but my efforts received barely a passing acknowledgement from you. I cannot please you…and I cannot try any more.

Once I came to this decision, I actually felt relief. At the same time, I wept knowing that my actions will destroy you, the one who was the center of my world for so long. I loved you. But I can't give you any more. I have a slow, painful journey ahead to reach the peace I need. The strength it took to take this final step came not from hating you, but from realizing that there is still goodness, hope and love left inside of me. I had to take this final action before it's too late for me to have any type of life worth living. I'm sorry, Jack. Goodbye.

Emma

There are moments in our lives that cause everything around us to fade to black. All we are left with is the continuous reel of the nightmare we just experienced, playing over and over in our mind. This was one of those moments for me. I could not move. I could not think. I felt a hurt growing in my chest that began spreading through my arms, into my neck, tensing my jaw, and moving towards my eyes, signaling the onset of tears. I had not seen this coming and the reality of it struck fast and hard. I could only sit, reeling from her words, struggling to understand all the feelings and emotions that ran through me, trying hard to avoid the facts I would have to face. I was going to be alone...without her...and I didn't know what I did wrong.

The first twenty-four hours after she left were sheer hell for me. I thought the night would never end, torturing me with the silence of the house and the lingering scent of her that still permeated the room and the bed. The bed I now slept in alone. The next morning, I attempted to reenter my old life, acting to those around me as if nothing had changed. I wanted so much to cry out, to cling to anyone who could share my pain and my loss. But there was no one. I learned that day that no matter how bad your heart is broken, the world doesn't stop for your grief. Only you can understand its depth, its breadth, and how much it affects you.

I spent the next several days, weeks, and months going through the motions of life. In that era, leaving someone was rare, and the isolation I had already imposed upon myself was worsened by the isolation I began to receive from others. He must have beat her, I imagined them saying in hushed tones *and knowing looks. He's a drunk, others would say in their gossip gaggles. No, speculated the wise, HE was having an affair and she must have found out. Poor, poor woman, they empathized. But they were wrong. All their reasoning, all their speculation, and all their gossip missed the true reason entirely. It was not what they said. The true reason she left was much worse than anything they could have imagined. She left because I gave her everything 'I' thought she needed….everything but me.*

One spring afternoon months later I was attending to business in a nearby city. I was very early for my appointment so I took a walk through the downtown area to pass the time. Ahead of me walked a young girl and her father, a relatively young man, and apparently one of reasonably good means. He seemed a bit lost with what to do with a young girl on a spring afternoon, so he was suggesting anything and everything that might be of interest.

"Would you like to go to the Woolworth's and get a fountain soda, Maggie?" he asked the little girl.

"No, Daddy."

"Well, what about the general store then. They have a lot of toys you can see. That would be fun, wouldn't it?"

"No, Daddy. I don't think so."

I could see his frustration starting to rise as a town of that size had limited options which could entertain a little girl, and temporarily relieve an uncomfortable father of the duty of making things interesting.

"We can't see a movie and we can't go very far since Mommy is with your little brother, so what do you want to do?" he asked, more frustrated than caring.

The little girl thought for a minute and said, "We don't have to do nothing, Daddy. Why don't you just hold my hand and we can walk around. Just be with me and love me."

Through the simple request of that little girl, I realized how badly I had failed Emma. I had simply not loved her in the way she wanted to be loved. I gave her everything I thought was important. Financial security, a home, food, and other material means. But not the simple things she needed the most, and probably the one thing she wanted the most: me. Sometimes all a person needs is a hand to hold and a heart to understand, but I had not given her any of that. I had given her everything but.

On the outside, you would have never known how Emma truly felt. I know I didn't. What confused me the most for so many months after she left was how perfect we seemed to be. We never argued. But if I am honest about it, it was not because we didn't disagree; it was because we didn't truly talk. Just because two people argue, it doesn't mean they don't love each other. And just because they don't argue, it doesn't mean they do. Yet I assumed the latter always meant they loved each other, and I was wrong.

As with any young love, we had started out hot and steamy, full of unbridled desire and longing for each other, with needs no one else could satisfy. But time will test a relationship, and as the passion fades there had better be something else to take its place. What I had assumed to be contentment and happiness after our first years together was likely just emptiness and hurt echoing in her heart. I had loved her in the only way I knew to love her, but sometimes that just isn't enough. You can't make someone love you in the way you think they should, nor make them appreciate the way that you love them. All you can do is be someone who can be loved.

I'm sorry, Emma. I truly am.

I had forgotten that my grandfather had been married before he met my grandmother. I had only stumbled upon this fact quite by accident when I, as a troublemaking boy of ten, and my 'willing to do whatever I did' cousin had burrowed into an old chest in my grandparents' attic and started pulling out letters, pictures, and all sorts of documents. A picture of my grandfather and some other woman had fallen to the floor and we had just picked it up when my mother appeared at the top of the attic stairs.

"WHAT ARE YOU BOYS DOING!" she cried.

"Mom! Look what we found! It's a picture of Grand-daddy and some woman. Who's that? Is it Grandmama?"

She snatched the picture from my hand and stared at it until the recognition flashed across her face.

"Wherever you got that, put that back NOW," she ordered. Mom glared at us until we had returned not only the picture, but the other contents of the chest, to their original places. Still under her frightening glare, we assumed our position in front of her like two AWOL soldiers preparing for corporal punishment. A few additional minutes of visual assault continued before she spoke.

"Don't ever let me catch you up here in your grandparents' things again. Do you hear me?"

Two bowed heads nodded silently in humble agreement.

"And don't you mention ANY of this to your grandparents...especially your grandmother. Do you understand?"

Another round of head nodding acknowledged the request.

We marched back down to the living room where every head turned and looked at us, unaware of the evil deed we had just committed...whatever it was. I saw my mother go over to my aunt and pull her into the kitchen for a private conversation. Her reaction mirrored my mother's although, quite honestly, I didn't fully understand what had happened.

On the ride home, and through dinner, my mother didn't say much to me at all. As she tucked me in for the night, I finally asked her who the mystery woman was.

"She was your grandfather's wife," my mother said, somewhat reluctantly. "From a long time ago."

I didn't say anything for minute.

"Where is she now? Did she die?"

Mother hesitated a little, thinking how to put this into words I could understand.

"She just went away and never came back. It made Granddaddy very sad, so we don't talk about it."

My ten year old brain pondered for a moment.

"You mean like Butch did?" Butch had been my little dog for many years, until he just disappeared one day.

"In a matter of speaking, yes. And do you remember how you felt when Butch went away?"

I nodded. I remembered how sad I felt and hoped my grandfather didn't feel that sad any more.

"That's why we don't talk about it. So Grandaddy won't be sad."

She kissed me goodnight and I fell off to sleep, content that I had the answer to the mystery of the lady in the picture.

Thirty-odd years later, I not only had insight into what exactly happened with the mysterious woman in the photograph, but I also had enough worldly knowledge to realize who the picture most likely would have upset: my grandmother. In those days, people remained married no matter what their situation or circumstance, so for him to be 'divorced' in an age of such social conservatism would have been quite a stigma. It would have held true both for him and for my grandmother, since she had been the 'second wife.' Every generation carries their insecurities, I suppose.

For me, I could relate to my grandfather's situation more than I initially realized. Whereas my grandfather was branded 'the divorced one,' I was branded 'the unmarried one.' In a family as small as mine, there is an unreasonable burden of keeping the family line going through the abundant production of offspring to bear the family name. One of my cousins, unfortunately for me, had married early and was already well into his planned family of five or six children. His 'achievement' was never allowed to wander far from my conscious mind—thanks to the efforts of my mother and my aunt. They would both ask (directly or indirectly) whether I had met any nice girls or if I had seen how pretty Kristin Strohm, my senior prom date who I never went out with again, had become. It was hard not to respond with some made-up lie that would give them something else to worry about other than my sperm count; like 'No, I don't like girls any more. I realized I am gay and am now dating a NFL lineman,' or 'I find I enjoy the convenience of prostitutes, as long as they take credit cards.' But I held back, patiently tolerating their well-meaning, but incredibly misguided, hints and suggestions.

My mother did have a small ray of hope a few years ago when I began spending time with, and apparently talking more about, Leigh Davidson. Leigh was the daughter of the founding partner of one of Atlanta's most prestigious law firms—Davidson and Findley—and was working through the ranks to partner in record time. She and I met one chilly December night at a charity event that her father's firm had sponsored at the Fernbank Museum. I had been cajoled into representing Associated Media at this annual high-society shindig. Donning tux and tie, I reluctantly sulked into the array of socialites to endure a few hours of their insincere bantering.

I had just taken a drink of my second glass of champagne when I felt a light touch on my shoulder.

"Excuse me, sir." I turned to look and found myself face to face with a beautiful stranger. "I'm afraid my earring is on the ground near your shoes and I just don't feel comfortable crawling around the feet of someone I don't know. Would you mind terribly retrieving it for me?" The request was closed with a captivating smile.

Leigh Davidson was the quintessential Southern debutante in the mold of a successful professional woman. With long blonde hair and clear blue eyes, she radiated a blend of confidence and allure without even the hint of effort. Though only in her late twenties, she was quickly following in her father's footsteps as a successful attorney. Tonight, however, the flowing black gown that accentuated her figure would make any man think of the bedroom well before the courtroom.

"While I would not protest any beautiful woman crawling around the floor beneath me, I will save you the embarrassment," I replied and bent down to retrieve what had to have been a 2 -carat diamond stud.

"Thank you" she said slowly, her eyes racing for recognition or recollection of a name.

"Aren't you..." I waited patiently, thinking I was about to be christened with a new name in a sad case of mistaken identity. "Carter Lee?"

"Why, yes." I said with a look of genuine surprise. "Have we met?"

She smiled with satisfaction at remembering my name, for whatever reason.

"Actually, no, we haven't. I'm Leigh Davidson. I'm a member of the Greater Midtown Development Council. I recall hearing you speak about how local corporations need to keep in mind Atlanta's architectural heritage when it comes to new projects. I thought it was an insightful point you raised."

I was impressed. That speech had been over two years ago and was a product of Mike's mandate that each of Associated Media's executives find a local cause to champion. I somehow ended up on a redevelopment committee for midtown Atlanta and had just run with the concept.

"Thanks," I said. I was hoping I could steer the conversation away from redevelopment since my attendance, and interest in, the concept had waned in recent months. "You must have an interest in older things...like me," I quipped, wondering if she'd pick up the double intent of my comment. She did.

Leigh laughed, and thus began a relationship that, though unexpected, seemed to combine the best of me with the best of her. We were like a perfect joint venture; our strengths supplemented the weaknesses of the other, making us quite an imposing team in the Atlanta social circle. Though both of us were consumed by our careers and our schedules, we would find moments or parties here and there where we could see each other and spend a few moments together. This went on for several months.

For me, it worked perfectly because I was in the midst of several key deal negotiations and just about every minute I had was structured to meet phone calls, web conferences, and day trips. My social obligations with Leigh rarely interfered with my work obligations, so everything was good. But Leigh, she was beginning to need more.

On a rainy April day at a luncheon she and I attended at the Westin, she broached the concept of maybe spending a few days away…together…without the cloud of a business or social purpose.

"I think Fripp Island would be a nice escape right about now," she whispered in my ear at a long table full of fellow corporate suits and attorneys, her hand gently grasping my arm. "Wouldn't it be nice to just be together with nothing in particular to do? Just the two of us."

What should have been an incredibly tempting offer from a woman to a man actually caused me to pass up the rest of my dessert. I had to admit I had become very comfortable with Leigh over the past several months and, in many ways, I felt a degree of affection for her that I had not often experienced. But what she suggested went to an entirely new place for us…for me. I felt she was encroaching on a private space to which she was not entitled, nor invited. I realized that 'intimate' was not how I viewed us.

Though from time-to-time we shared companionship

and simple touches that went beyond mere friendship, I was not any more in love with this woman today than I was on the day I first met her. But apparently she was developing feelings for me that extended well beyond anything I thought I could feel for her. In reaction to this, I felt myself withdrawing from, or opting out of, any element of interaction that went beyond merely casual. Suddenly, I could not make events we had agreed to attend together months earlier, my business trips became more frequent and lengthy, and my availability by phone dropped off to nil. Even lunch together became difficult to schedule for me. I just didn't feel comfortable going where she wanted to go.

This went on for weeks. Finally, one day I received a rather pointed email from Leigh asking me to meet her at the Capital Grill in Buckhead at 6:00 that night as she had something she needed to tell me. I cringed at the request, but resigned myself to the obligation as I had put-off and stonewalled her at least three times within the past week. Leigh was waiting for me when I arrived, a glass of water the only item in front of her. Without a word, she motioned for me to have a seat. I complied.

"I'll be brief, Carter. It's obvious you are no longer as interested in me or us as you were in the past. I'm pretty upset by the way you've been treating me considering I'm not sure what I did that suddenly made you feel like we could not continue as we were. If you don't want this to go anywhere, that's fine. I just wish you would have told me."

Her legal persona was in effect and I was very uncomfortable as the object of her cross-examination.

"Since you apparently do not have the guts to do it, I just wanted to tell you that I won't be calling you, emailing you, or expecting anything from you anymore...from this point forward. I could have just disappeared, but that's not who I am, Carter. So, I appreciate you meeting me here tonight so we can wrap this up."

The next few minutes encompassed one of the longer silences I could recall in my life as I waited for her to say something else...anything to fill the silence. Finally, I asked a question.

"Are you breaking up with me, Leigh?" I knew I was stating the obvious, but since I was hoping for closure on the inevitable, I felt I had to ask.

For a second her eyes showed surprise at my question, but immediately refocused. She gave me a look that was a mix of sadness and contempt.

"Carter," she said slowly, "you broke up with me a long time ago. I'm just making it official. Goodbye, Carter." With that, she quietly gathered up her purse and coat and left the bar without looking back, leaving me with a strange feeling of relief and failure.

No matter what a man's station in life, nothing is more demoralizing than being told by a woman that you can no longer be tolerated. It's a hurtful, horrible message to receive. My grandfather received his one day long ago through a pen and paper narrative waiting for him on his kitchen table. Mine had come via a few simple statements by a Vera Wang-ensconced professional sitting across from me in an overpriced bar in Buckhead. It doesn't matter how the message arrives however, the effect on a man's psyche is always the same.

Granted, I had engineered my own fate in this case. I had become quite adept over the years at bringing even the most promising of relationships to failure, and I could only admit I had followed my modus operandi with Leigh. She didn't deserve it and I, from the beginning, did not deserve her. So as if to fulfill my seemingly repetitive obligation to help the fates be right, I chalked up another tick on the headboard of the bed of loneliness I made for myself time after miserable time.

As much as I hated to read the heartbreak my grandfa-

ther had endured, it gave me a degree of comfort that this
man, whom all seemed to love and adore, could have failed
so miserably at the affairs of the heart. To have the chance to
read his words and to 'hear' him enunciate his pain, was a
rare look into the private world of a man's heart. For when
men experience heartbreak, they bear the pain alone. Unlike
the ability of women to bend the ear of a confidant at the
first whisper of love gone bad, men generally have no one
in which to confide. Because of my dedication to work over
the years, I had engendered no support network, no male
friends, no sympathetic ear to which I could plead my case.
Even if I had, though, it's not a topic that is easily received
or truly understood within the circle of men. A look of 'I'm
sorry' or 'Damn, that sure sucks' are the typical segues to a
completely different topic…one without discomfort for the
listener, and benign enough for the heartbroken to potentially take his mind off of 'her.' At least, that's the hope. But
rarely does it work, and we suffer silently, alone in the
company of men.

It was a common point we now shared, my grandfather
and I. My grandfather had ultimately found love with my
grandmother, but the question whether I could ever get
beyond 'me' to be a part of 'we' still lingered. In a life full of
achievement and success, it was not something I dwelled on,
but from time-to-time, during moments of reflection such as
this, the failures and their pain would come to the forefront
of my mind. No one wants to die alone, but as the years
passed by, I could hear the voice of fate reminding me of the
possibility.

Jessica crossed my mind at that moment, as if to offer a
competing view of my future and what it could hold. But
reading my grandfather's narrative in the dim light had
made me drowsy, and sleep was quickly overtaking me. She
would be a thought for another day, I told myself as I
drifted off for the night.

THURSDAY

Thursday morning found Jessica Cooper showered and nursing her first cup of coffee at the kitchen table by 7:30 a.m., staring absentmindedly out the big bay window. She was going to need an extra cup or two this morning before she could engage the day, but the jolt of caffeine was slowly clearing the bleariness from her head. It HAD been a shorter night than she was used to having. By 9:30 each night, she was usually in bed watching television or nursing one of the three novels she had going at any one time. Her routine had conditioned her body to expect an entitlement of at least nine hours of sleep per night, so any deviation from that schedule was duly noted.

It was not the lateness of last evening that drained her energy, however. It had been the thoughts and feelings racing through her mind and heart that had kept her in a restless state for most of the night. Jessica knew herself very well and, over the course of last evening, she could feel a connection growing with Carter. She was not one to give in so easily to another, but something about Carter Lee met a need in her that she could not put her finger on. Whatever the connection was, it was very real to her.

Her restlessness was brought on by the enduring strug-gle between her rational mind and the tug of her heart.

Jessica had seemingly endless compassion and empathy towards the feelings of others, but she did not always allow herself the same nurturing. Not that she needed anyone, mind you. Jessica had moved through life on the wind of success, accomplishing more than even she had expected. She didn't NEED anyone. But no heart can truly admit that solitude is the preferred state of being, and Jessica's was no exception.

There had been men in her life. The first, and most dear, was her father. Sandy Cooper had been the type of father a girl dreamt of having: patient, kind, thoughtful, yet very clear about his expectations of her AND the expectations she should have of others. When she was younger, she didn't fully understand the meaning of respect and consideration. But later in life, she grasped how he was building her up to be a strong, independent woman, an unexpected blessing from a father in that day and age. He was taken from her much too early, and though her mother had tried to fill the void, it was never really the same. In their short time together, Sandy had made the most of each moment with Jessica. He left an indelible mark on his daughter's life that was exclusively his own, and she would miss him for the rest of her days.

Over the years, she had on occasion met, liked, loved, and parted with a few other special men. Each had brought her a new understanding of love and its caveats, though none had ever been anyone she could not live without. Jessica had been blessed with many male friends, however, and it was nice to have the company and presence of a man in a platonic setting from time-to-time. Brian, her boss in D.C., had been one of those friends, but just before her mother became ill it had felt as if he wanted to overstep the boundaries of his marriage—with her. Maybe it had all been in her imagination, but subtle comments and sharing of details from his personal life, beyond anything she had any interest in knowing, had caused her to reduce the amount of contact they had or the one-on-one situations in which they found themselves. Being the 'other woman' was not a place she was willing to go, and she ensured she would not be placed in that situation.

In recent years, her life had experienced more goodbyes than hellos, which after awhile makes one simply stop trying. Jessica had begun to accept that she may simply be too independent of a spirit to connect with a man on an intimate emotional level, and that was OK. Everything of the heart seemed fraught with complications for her, despite her best efforts. But this time, something felt different.

Her initial reaction to Carter Lee was not positive, and somewhere in the back of her mind lingered a fear or a caution about him. As she began to know him, however, she became more dismissive of this reaction. It was more like the typical argument of logic she encountered with her inner self rather than anything substantive she could identify. If anything, Carter's openness in his words and thoughts portrayed a man unlike any she had known before. He had given her insight into the struggle he had caring for the dying grandfather he hardly knew. A struggle not from the frustration of inconvenience, but from the emptiness of not knowing the man he admired and respected any more than he did. Carter did not pour out his heart to gain her sympathy; he simply wanted her to know the person he was. She liked that, as well as how receptive he was to her thoughts and the private details she shared with him. It was nice, as simple as it sounds. Jessica found herself longing to again sit beside Carter and see where their time together would lead.

Carter backed slowly out of the driveway and onto the gravel road before turning the wheel towards the Sweet

Branch Hospice Center. The road was empty on this peaceful autumn morning, and though it was a stark contrast to his old life in Atlanta, he was slowly acclimating to the pace and schedule of life in Sweet Branch. He had given up his higher-end casual wear and instead opted for his faded jeans, an old pair of work boots, and a khaki denim work shirt he had borrowed from his grandfather's closet that morning. It wasn't that his borrowed attire was necessarily more comfortable, but he just didn't feel like himself in his old wardrobe any longer.

He had taken his coffee out to the back porch again, just to enjoy a few minutes of the peaceful morning and to visit with Brown Dog, who seemed to be most inclined to do her visiting in the early morning. He enjoyed her company more and more each time as it reminded him of his childhood dog, Butch. Men and dogs share a special connection and for Carter, Brown Dog was a welcome confidant in the present. They had spent the best part of an hour together when Carter realized he needed to leave before the morning became any older.

Several more journals, the binder, and his cell phone were collected in his backpack and slung over his shoulder when he noticed his Blackberry sitting on the counter. He hesitated, then held the power button down until the start-up sequence initiated. After a few seconds, the familiar taunting of 'NO SERVICE' glared back at him from the upper right hand corner. Where earlier in the week the lack of service would have agitated his already delicate psyche, this rebuttal actually brought him a sense of relief. He tossed the Blackberry to the counter and headed out the door. In his head, he mused an apology of sorts to Mike as he was completely out of touch at this point. Mike likely had everything running better than ever, Carter reasoned. But how wrong he was.

"Dammit, Carter. Where are you?"

Mike Booker pushed away his keyboard in disgust after checking his email for what seemed like the millionth time over the past few days. He needed to talk to Carter, and soon. Though his decision to put Carter on an involuntary sabbatical had seemed like a good idea at the time, he had quickly realized how ingrained, and critical, Carter was to the many high dollar projects he controlled. London was calling with questions on a past asset sale. Investors in Tokyo were offering up a tremendous equity opportunity that had an exploding deadline. Western U.S. operations needed direction on some contract language. Why in the hell did he pick THIS week to slow Carter down?

Granted, Carter, and moreover, Carter's department, needed a break. Though a genuinely nice individual with a good heart, Carter Lee could drive a person to the very limits of their capabilities, sometimes beyond what should be possible. His teams always delivered, and several mid-level managers who had survived his tutelage were already showing tremendous potential as they scattered out across Associated Media. But some of the results were coming at a high price. Turnover in the professional ranks was increasing, and it was not a pleasant task for Mike to explain to senior leadership why their $100K+ Ivy League MBAs were bailing out for opportunities elsewhere. Much of the turnover had come out of Carter's group and, without intervention, Mike did not see anything changing. He did what he thought was right.

Mike worried about Carter personally, as well. Though in the latter stages of a very successful career, Mike Booker had kept his life reasonably balanced between a demanding corporate role and a family of five. If a road show required him to be away for a week or two, he would take a few days off to catch up with his brood. He made sure he was as integral to them as he was to Associated Media. Business trips sometimes doubled as vacations, and he and Sarah let very little impinge on their Tuesday date night. Maybe date night meant hot dogs and warm soda at one of their son's baseball games or a double cheeseburger enroute to their daughter's ballet recital, but it still counted as special time. Sarah and the kids had been his anchor for much of his adult life, and he intended to be theirs as well.

Carter, however, didn't seem to have such an anchor. Mike hired Carter right out of the University of South Carolina's IMBA program and, from the start, they had a father/son-like relationship. Mike coached, developed, and mentored Carter his entire career and both knew each others' styles innately. One thing Mike had never done was exercise his power and influence to move Carter into increasing levels of responsibility. He didn't have to. Carter's style and success took care of that all by itself. Over the years, Carter had showed tremendous dedication to the company's success and had put in more effort than any executive Mike had ever known. The powers that be recognized that and acted accordingly.

But what haunted Mike was how intertwined Carter and his job seemed to be. On the rare occasions when they had the chance to talk alone outside of the office, Carter would inevitably find a way to swing the topic back to a business discussion. A recent Falcon's loss morphed into ideas around product placement and advertising opportunities. Mike's vacation to the Basque Coast led to a discussion around a potential opportunity in the neighboring country of Portugal. It just went on and on, and like anyone with a sense of paternal obligation, Mike had noticed this for a long time, but wasn't sure what to do.

The issue pushed to a head, however, when less experienced employees in Carter's group began to resign. Associated Media had invested quite a bit of time and effort into recruiting and hiring these individuals for future needs, and the exit interviews from Human Resources all pointed a finger at Carter's style of management. Complaints ranged from too much stress and long hours, to expectations of weekend work and the lack of any meaningful feedback. Twenty years ago, Mike could have just said 'That's life. Tough it out.' But today's labor market, especially for high-quality MBAs, was in favor of the students. They had choices and if they didn't like what you had to offer, they would leave…and they told their friends back at their top-notch B-schools WHY they were leaving. A bad reputation is not something Mike could live with.

He had decided late last week that Carter needed some time away, hopeful that a complete disconnect would right the ship a little. Though he still needed Carter's contributions, he needed Carter to find something else in life to interest him, to keep him from running everyone, including himself, into the ground. But he had not expected Carter to vanish like he had. Though he promised not to respond to emails, Carter had always shown a penchant for insubordination when it was in the best interest of the business. Mike fully expected Carter to call in, or at least respond to one tempting email, by midweek, today at the latest. But nothing.

After another check of his inbox, Mike hollered to his assistant, his quasi-work spouse.

"Terri. Can you PLEASE see if you can reach Carter by either email or cell phone? Call his damn mother if you have to. I need to speak with him NOW, and he won't respond to my emails or voicemails."

Terri rolled her eyes at her desk, knowing Mike couldn't see her.

"Do you want me to reactivate his Blackberry service and cell phone?"

Mike blinked.

"Do I want you to do what?"

Terri sighed and went over to his doorway.

Very clearly she said, "Reactivate his Blackberry service and his cell phone. It's been turned off since he left on Monday."

"TURNED OFF? WHO THE HELL TURNED OFF HIS SERVICE?"

"I did."

She couldn't help but enjoy this. Mike worked himself up terribly over the littlest things, and this would likely send him into orbit.

"YOU DID? WHY DID YOU DO THAT?" Crimson was creeping up his neck and into his cheeks.

"Because you told me to," Terri responded with a slight smile.

"I did?" Mike cocked his head and gave her his typical blank look. He was a brilliant leader but his short-term memory was a completely different matter.

"Yes. You did. You said that Carter needed to be completely disconnected from work and that we should consider shutting off his service. So I did."

Mike frowned. "I thought I meant we should consider it..." The words trailed off as he feigned looking for something on his desk. Maybe he did tell Terri to turn off Carter's service. He couldn't remember. No wonder Carter wasn't responding. He couldn't.

"Would you like me to see if he has a personal cell number or some other contact information in his file?"

"Yes...yes....or an email...maybe we have a personal email...or something...."

"Yes, sir. I'll take care of that."

Terri turned slowly from the door and lowered her face so no one would see her smiling.

That made my entire day, she thought to herself.

Carter arrived at the hospice center a little bit after 9:00 a.m. He waved to the receptionist as he walked in, receiving a friendly 'Mornin', Mr. Lee' in response. As he made his way to his grandfather's room, he nodded to the son of the resident in room 150 next door and waved down the hall to the LPN who was slowly making her way to give Jack Bailey his daily sponge bath.

"Hey, there, Mr. Lee," Connie Leonard offered. "It's time for his sponge bath and change." In his state, Jack Bailey had lost all control of his bodily functions, making an adult diaper a necessity. "Would you want to help out or anything?"

"Oh, no. You go right ahead. I'll just wait out here until you're done," Carter responded, a little too quickly he realized.

He had become comfortable with his role as caregiver for the week, but the thought of becoming too familiar with his grandfather's personal cleanliness was well beyond his comfort level. Carter had gained a new respect for how Jessica made a living, even if she wasn't the one who usually had to handle some of the more unpleasant tasks. Dealing with human beings on such a basic level intimidated him. In his world, people were salaries, headcounts, and factors of production, but in Jessica's world they were very human, very real components of her everyday job.

Carter was leaning against the wall outside Jack's room pondering all of this when he saw Jessica walking down the hall. Even from a distance, every gentle sway of her body had his full attention. The closer she got to him, the more the professional demeanor gave way to the personal demeanor that was attracting Carter more and more.

"Good morning, Mr. Lee," she smiled, feigning a hint of formality for the benefit of whomever may be within earshot.

"Good morning to you, Ms. Cooper," he replied. "Always nice to see you." He winked, acknowledging her jest. "I trust you're having a good morning?"

Jessica rolled her eyes then leaned within earshot.

"Not really. Must be a full moon. Everyone is in a mood. Plus, I think one of my favorite patients is giving up. That always makes me sad."

"I'm sorry. That doesn't sound like it makes for a very good day," he offered. Carter liked the feeling of her intimately confiding in him.

"No, it certainly doesn't. But that's just part of the job," she said with a slight shrug. "Why are you out here in the hall?"

"Personal care time for my grandfather," he offered, trying to sound casual. "Figured I'd give him some privacy."

But Jessica knew better.

"You just didn't want anything to do with that, did you?" she countered.

"Eh, no. Not so much," he grinned. "That's just not a place I think I can go."

"I don't blame you," she conceded. "There is a line sometimes as to how familiar family wants to get. Men especially seem to shy away from all that." She changed the subject. "So, are you still interested in coming over for dinner tonight?"

"Yes, if it still works for you. I really appreciate the offer. I've been thinking about it since last night." Dinner had been a part of his thoughts, but by no means was it the only topic.

"Absolutely. Be there at 6:00 or thereabouts." She pulled a pad from her coat pocket, scribbled her address and a few directions, and handed it to him. "It's not hard to find, but I gave you both directions and the address in case you wanted to use your GPS gizmo."

Carter reached out for the directions and intentionally let

the grasp of his hand linger. She caught his gaze.

"Thank you for last night. I really had a nice time with you," he said simply.

Carter noticed a hint of pink in Jessica's cheeks as she acknowledged his words.

"Thanks, Carter, I did, too...and I'm really looking forward to tonight."

They lingered again as they had earlier in the week, only this time it wasn't for a lack of anything to say, but a hesitancy to let go.

"I guess I should finish my rounds..."

He stood up slowly from the wall as the door to his grandfather's room opened.

"OK. I guess we both have to get back to work now..."

Jessica smiled.

"I'll check in on you in a little bit," she said as she turned and walked away, glancing quickly around to see if anyone noticed the smile she could not hide.

Connie was packing her supplies and putting the soiled towels and linens in the hamper as Carter took his seat alongside the bed.

"I think he's set now, at least for another couple of hours," she said. "I changed his pads and sponged him down, but I'll come back tomorrow to shave him. You have a good day, Mr. Lee."

Carter looked at his grandfather, neatly positioned in the bed and as still as a statue.

"I will, Connie. Thanks so much for your help."

The room smelled of soap and fresh linen, a nice change from the usual whiffs of antiseptic and other sanitary products used throughout the center. Except for the occasional murmur of voices and televisions from the surrounding rooms, it was quiet and peaceful in the space he and Jack shared.

Over the years, Carter had not understood the need to be

with someone in a state like the one in which his grandfather was currently living. It seemed unnecessary to burden
the time of the living with an obligation to the sick, ill, and
dying unless there was a particular purpose provided. In
this case, there was none. Jack Bailey was not going to get
any better. Even if there was some type of medical expertise
that could help him, Carter was not the one who could
provide it.

But in the stillness, Carter sensed his grandfather...much
like the heat radiating softly around a light bulb. The heat is
subtle, but it's there. If Carter could sense him and knew
there was at least an animate being within range of him,
maybe his grandfather, in some small way, knew equally
that Carter was there—for him—in this place. Carter may
never know if his grandfather felt his presence, but at least
for now, he understood why just being here held a meaning
for those he called his family.

He settled back in the chair and began to inventory the
journals he brought for the day. Luckily, the first journal he
had chosen on Tuesday was the first journal his grandfather
had ever written, so he had not violated the sequence
dictated on the little yellow pages. He found himself right
on schedule. The next sequence of journals Carter was to
read began right after Emma had left his grandfather and
appeared to continue well through most of his grandfather's
life. Though it was a span of many years, they were of such
interest to Carter that he read without ceasing for most of
the day, stopping only for bathroom breaks and to chat with
Jessica as she made her rounds.

To Carter, it was a fascinating synopsis of a lifetime. At
the beginning of the section, his grandfather covered the
pain of Emma's leaving, his immersion into his work on the
farm and in his businesses, and the questions of life that
crossed his mind on occasion. From time-to-time, Carter
sensed a regret hanging in his grandfather's thoughts, as if

he had missed an opportunity or squandered a chance. Though it was unclear what the situation might have been, or if it was only Carter's inference.

Soon Jack began to speak of a new woman in his life, the woman who would become Carter's grandmother. While familiar with his own thought process about women, he had never considered how other men may think or how similarly or dissimilarly their feelings and considerations were from his own. He and his grandfather shared surprisingly similar thoughts in the early stages of a relationship, but also some obvious differences. Both shared the same hopes, fears, and questions about the opposite sex, and to Carter's amusement, asked the same questions about the workings of the feminine mind. But where his grandfather considered the traditional notions of motherhood and domestic abilities, Carter considered intellectual engagement and her independent nature. His grandfather wondered about her family and the religious beliefs they held; whereas, Carter desired insight into how well her drive and ambition mirrored his own. It was the generation gap personified.

Carter's grandmother had been a blessing to the wayward life of Jack Bailey, and the change in the mood of his grandfather's writings was obvious the moment she entered his world. It was intriguing to see how their relationship matured, transitioning into their roles of husband and wife and father and mother to their two girls. Hearing him describe Carter's mother as a young child, including the peculiar and frustrating things children are apt to do, put his mother in an entirely new light. Carter thought his grandfather had been blessed with a peaceful, contented life, and it seemed he valued and treasured every moment of it.

Carter finished the last journal in the sequence late in the afternoon and set it on the floor beside him. Leaning back in the chair, he closed his eyes and let the pictures, recollections, and memories from a lifetime that predated his own settle in his mind. Though captivated by this plethora of information that was uniquely his family, it drained him both physically and emotionally. He wanted to understand and retain every thread of history his grandfather's writings conveyed. He was no longer reading just to pass the time; instead, he was trying to create a semblance of the relationship he never had with his grandfather.

After a time, he remembered he still had one more chronicle of information awaiting him: the yellow pages in the small binder. He reached into his backpack, pulled out the narrative, and turned to section #2 for what he now viewed as his grandfather's look back at that portion of his life.

When I was young, there was a circuit preacher in our area named Preacher Sam. Being a circuit preacher wasn't the most lucrative of ways to make a living, so Preacher Sam was a full-time farmer, as well. Preacher Sam lived on a hundred or so acre tract across the river from our land, on which he raised rows and rows of different varieties of apple trees. In the fall, my brothers and I worked for Preacher Sam in the orchards when our own crops were in the barn awaiting the coming winter, or off to market for sale. When you have a hundred acres of apple trees, there is plenty of work to go around.

One might think that a preacher would be the kindest, gentlest boss in the world, whose every word dripped with the grace and caring of our beloved Heavenly Father. Far from it. Preacher Sam was the most demanding task master I ever experienced in all my years of working. Ingrained with the belief that teenage boys are naturally disposed to goofing-off when there is work to be done, Preacher made sure we were always busy and focused on whatever he had charged us to do. It was not unlike him to utilize management skills that bordered on sadistic, if not down right mean.

One afternoon I was up high in a tree picking apples when I decided I'd take a break. Not a long break, mind you, but long enough to enjoy a few minutes of mindless daydreaming on a fall afternoon. I was about halfway through my self-awarded break when...WHAP. The impact of something round and hard sent waves of searing heat and pain across my back that pulsed with each beat of my now racing heart. I had to grab the tree to keep the ladder from falling, the heavy sack of apples I wore across my chest now acting as a life-saving counterbalance.

"What the..." I said out loud to no one in particular as I whirled around to see what, or who, had decided to attack me for no apparent reason.

"GIT BACK TO WORK, BOY!" came Preacher's growl from somewhere below me. "You think I'm payin' you good dollar to pontificate on God's handiwork up there on that ladder? Do that on yer own time. God ain't never gonna charge you for lookin', but He's not payin' you, either. I AM." From that point forward, I never let Preacher see me taking a break again because, quite honestly, I didn't like getting chastised by the man. He could take your ego to the bottom of the deepest pit and leave it there for days.

But just as sweet balances sour, Preacher Sam was balanced in life by Ruby, his wife of many years. She was a gentle soul; a blend of kindness, consideration, and soft words that complemented the crass, fiery, and hard character that comprised her mate. And could she cook. On Saturdays when my brothers and I would work a full day bringing in apples by the bushel, she prepared a noon-time spread that made the weight of the work and the glare of Preacher Sam all worth it. Fried chicken, pole beans, succotash, fresh tomatoes, corn on the cob, mashed potatoes, country ham, biscuits, and some of the best chocolate pie I ever had. All washed down, of course, by apple cider kept cold in the spring house just down from the main house. It was heavenly to the insatiable appetite of a young man, and even after a full afternoon of work, that lunch would stick with you *like a hug from a good friend.*

Years passed and we eventually stopped working on Preacher Sam's farm. My brothers entered into their own obligations and families, as did I, and Preacher Sam sold off most of his orchards, except for a few small acres that adjoined his house. You could still hear the fiery voice of God's messenger blazing out the windows of his circuit churches on any given Sunday, but the remaining days of the week were spent in quiet reflection with his wife...his friend...his soul mate. Together they would hold hands on the front porch of that old farmhouse and watch God's world change from season to season to season. It was a show that seemed offered for their pleasure only, and they treasured each moment they had left together to enjoy it.

Over the years, Preacher Sam's body began the inevitable journey down the road of old age. Feet that previously pounded confidently across the wooden floors of the many churches on his circuit now treaded lightly and cautiously. It was harder for him to rise from, and sit down in, his favorite chair, but even harder to ask for help in doing so. While his wife's body traveled the same difficult and final road as his, her mind was also going along for the ride. She began to suffer bouts of forgetfulness that became periods of confusion and chaos, and she eventually lived in a permanent state of what we now call dementia. She was completely unable to care for herself and, without any children of their own to help, Preacher Sam saw himself as the one...the ONLY one...who would take care of Ruby's every need.

Families from the community dropped in on Preacher Sam and Ruby more and more frequently. Partly to drop off care baskets of bread, garden vegetables, and whatever else they thought might be of help, but also to beg Preacher Sam to accept their assistance in caring for Ruby. To the person asking, the answer was always the same: "No, no. It ain't necessary. We don't need no one goin' outta their way for us. God bless your heart for offerin', but we'll be fine. Thanks much."

This went on for months and months. Concern mounted for Ruby's (and Preacher's) well-being to a point of adamant panic. After all, was it Christian to let two people who absolutely could not care for themselves continue to live alone to the detriment of one or both of them? It just did not seem right.

Before a prayer circle could be formed to ask for God Almighty's assistance to sway a bent of stubbornness that only He could have created in a man, word came that Preacher Sam had called for the doctor to come quickly. Apparently, Ruby was failing—and failing fast—so Preacher Sam did the only thing he knew to do when it came to things of medicine—call the doctor. I passed Dr. Debusk on my way home and he asked if I would come along with him. I didn't mind, and he needed someone to distract Preacher Sam while he examined Ruby. Preacher Sam was fiercely protective over her and he would not leave her side, no matter what.

We arrived at Preacher's house about 20 minutes later and knocked loudly on the door. Preacher's hearing was never good to begin with, probably due to the volume he used belting out his Sunday messages over the years, but what he didn't hear, Ruby usually did. But she could not watch out for him like that any longer. The door opened and a tired, haggard face with sad eyes met our gaze.

"Gentlemen." Preacher said as he motioned us to come in. The man who had intimidated me so much in my youth had been reduced to a diminutive figure barely three quarters of my size. The once bellowing voice was barely audible over the shuffling of his leather-soled work shoes. The flannel shirt that covered his gaunt frame appeared to be a size or two too large, and if it wasn't for suspenders, the man's pants didn't have a chance of staying up around his waist.

"Ruby's restin' back in the bedroom, Doc." Preacher eyed me as if to say, 'you stay here with me.' Only Doc went, which was completely fine with me. With all the attention paid to

Ruby by the town, I was wondering who was paying any attention to Preacher Sam. I was more than glad to visit for awhile.

We moved over to the sitting area, a front room filled with more wingbacks and love seats than would be required for just the two of us. It was our first meeting in several years, so without any recent history of which to speak, our conversation was somewhat awkward at first. In true Preacher Sam fashion, however, he immediately cut to his first thought.

"You're older."

I couldn't help but smile at his opening statement, considering my first thought of him was how time had changed him as well.

"Yes, Preacher, I am. I'm not sure I could climb those apple trees for you like I used to."

"Well, ain't no big loss," he said quietly, his eyes giving away a hint of disinterest in our topic. "Some fellars ain't cut out for hard work."

Though the years had taken a lot of the fire away from him, Preacher could still take my ego down a notch or two. These days, however, I wore a much thicker skin and could take his observations without the spike of angst I experienced as a much younger man. My ability to engage him in conversation was already waning, so I turned the topic to the one I felt would be most dear to his heart.

"How is Ruby doing?"

His eyes took on a bit more life with that question and he straightened up, as well as he could, in the wingback chair.

"She's none too good. The doc comes to visit once or twice a week, I reckon, without me havin' to call him. 'Checkin' up,' he says, which is good. I figure he just has some slow spots in his day and thinks a walk out this way would do him good." His voice had a much more caring, yet serious, tone akin to the nature of his care-giving task.

I didn't say anything.

"But not good, I don't reckon. I was thinkin' I needed to call him today when she wouldn't take her mornin' or midday meals." He fidgeted with the ornate curls on the arm of the chair as he pondered his next words.

"She may be goin' home soon."

Where I grew up, people didn't die. They simply 'went home' or 'passed on,' as most believed death was not an end. In his way, and in the way of his culture, he was telling me that Ruby was about to go to Heaven...away from him.

We sat in silence, letting his words have their moment.

"Do you think that would be best at this point? She's had it rough for the last few years. The Ruby we know hasn't been here in awhile...," I offered quietly.

The woman Preacher Sam knew had died many years previous, as her mind could no longer associate what was real from what was in her memory. For decades Ruby had been his strength, but slowly their roles had changed. Soon it was he who buttoned her sweater when her withered fingers failed, the one who read her the letters from far away relatives and distant friends, and the one who held her as she wept when she could no longer remember his name. Time had taken Sam's wife, but it could not take away his love. His last duties as a husband were to write the closing chapter of their Earthly relationship, reflecting on memories and saying what could not be left unspoken, to prepare her for the long journey that death would soon require. There was no question in my mind that, even now, he was more in love with her than any man could ever be. I could not even begin to understand what he was going through.

He looked at me without saying anything.

"Preacher...you did everything you could. No one could have done as well as you did taking care of her. I don't know how you did all that you did, to be honest."

Whether it was the acknowledgement that someone had seen the meaning behind his acts of love for Ruby in her last days, or the stark realization that Ruby's life was indeed winding down, I'll never know. All I know is that a solitary tear began making its way down his weathered cheek as he lowered his head. Preacher Sam gently stroked the worn gold band on his left ring finger as if recalling the moment she put it on his finger...the moment they became husband and wife.

"Don't seem like all that long ago we wed," he whispered. "Do it all over again if I could. She was my girl..." His now sorrowful eyes met mine. "She was my girl."

That afternoon, Ruby passed away.

The same process he had led so many times before was now set in motion for Preacher Sam. He went through the motions of the service, nodding thanks to the many participants in attendance to say their goodbyes, and gratefully accepting the many gifts of food brought through the kitchen. When the house was finally empty and mourners had returned to their own lives, the silence must have been overwhelming. He may have sat in the musty parlor, straining for the sounds of slow, shuffling feet across the oak floors, for a raspy voice mumbling about days gone by, or soft snoring from her faded, worn chair...for anything to represent life in the house. But only silence met him. Ruby was gone.

Preacher Sam had joined the multitude of those whose common bond was the void of loss. He knew Ruby was dying, but the loss of her love, a love which had always been present in his life, took away his last connection to her and what they had been. Her passing must have been more than Preacher's poor broken heart could bear, for he died a few days after they laid her in the ground. Many times death brings sadness, but in Preacher Sam's case, it was a blessing that he didn't have to wait...alone...to see her again. Sometimes life is funny that way.

After Emma left me, I struggled with her loss and seriously wondered if I could ever be a man that any woman would want. I had already made one significant mistake in my life...not *being able to see past myself to give Emma the only thing she really wanted: me. Some folks never get one chance to have someone special in their life; I had had mine and had thrown it away. Maybe I was destined to be alone. I had spent so much time in the deep recesses of my own despair that I had forgotten what it felt like to live. I was more able to associate with Preacher Sam's sense of death and dying than anything associated with life and light. But like I said, life is funny sometimes, as that's when I met Elizabeth.*

Elizabeth Wheeler had come to our small town to replace the retiring elementary school teacher, Ms. Eugenia Birch. Ms. Birch had been educator and quasi-parent to most of us who had remained in and around the area, so her moving on was a milestone in all of our lives. I was asked if I would pick up Ms. Wheeler when her train arrived from Knoxville one Saturday since I owned a farm truck that would be more than adequate for hauling all of her belongings to Mrs. Owen's boarding house. To this day I remember the first moment I saw her at the station: chestnut brown hair, coal-black eyes, and a warm smile that made me literally forget who I was or why I was even there.

Elizabeth found a man completely exposed to the very basis of who he was: no flash, no shine, not much to offer at all. But maybe that's why we worked—I was who I was. She fell in love with the true me. That was all I ever had to be with Elizabeth and I, simply put, fell in love with her. Together, we became greater than what we individually could have ever been. She helped me learn and understand the things that truly mattered and never gave up on me when I just didn't get it the first time...or the second time...or the third time.

Elizabeth taught me how to trust without suspicion, to accept gifts and compliments with an open heart and mind. That being forgetful and living in the moment helps one to 'forgive and forget.' That just because someone doesn't love you the way you want them to doesn't mean they don't love you with all they have. There are people who love you dearly, but just don't know how to show it. That the for-richer-or-poorer, for-better-or-worse aspects of marriage don't hit you right away; it's only during those rare times when we take stock of our life that it starts to sink in. That there are many ways of falling and staying in love. That our background and circumstances may have influenced who we are, but we are responsible for who we become. That maturity has more to do with what types of experiences you've had and what you've learned from them and less to do with how many birthdays you've celebrated. One last thing I learned from my life with Elizabeth was that the people you care most about in life are taken from you way too soon and that you should always leave loved ones with loving words. It may be the last time you see them.

It was supposed to be a simple trip to the store for bread since some of the family were coming over for Sunday dinner. I wasn't gone long, but it didn't take long for her to go. I arrived home to find my love of 46 years laying not far from where she waved goodbye to me just thirty minutes before. The doctor said it was an aneurysm and that she didn't suffer, but none of that mattered to me. She was gone, and I felt that pain of loss that only I could understand. I thanked God, though, that before I walked out that door, before I kissed her cheek for the final time, she was able to look in my eyes and see the love that I felt for her. If nothing else, that would not be a question for her heart to have to ponder as she waited for me on the other side of the light.

Unlike times past when I lamented my own mistakes or ached for what I should have done differently, I simply miss Elizabeth's presence in my life. I think that's what tells me it was so right and that I finally figured it out…with her love and help. And that's OK. I know someday I will see her again and that we will simply pick up where we left off those years ago. I only hope that she understands that—

And then it stopped.

"Understands WHAT?" Carter muttered to himself, exasperated at yet another dangling thought.

"Are you talking to yourself?" a voice from the door asked. Jessica was leaning against the doorway, arms folded around several brown binders.

Carter looked up with a frown.

"Actually I was talking to him," he whispered quietly, motioning his thumb towards the motionless figure in the bed. "He's leaving me with more questions than answers in some of his writings."

Jessica moved towards the bed, still clutching the medical records like a schoolgirl carries her books.

"I just wanted to let you know I'm going to kick out a little early, once I finish my notes for the day. I just came by to check Jack…er…your grandfather one more time." She looked at the arrangement of journals he had scattered around his chair. "Can I help you with any of that?" she asked.

Carter blushed then shook his head.

"No, but thanks, though. I need to put them back in order, I think." He started loading journals back into his bag. "I'm almost finished here myself. I did a huge amount of reading today so I should probably decompress before I come over. Otherwise, I may be as dull as house dust."

"Somehow I doubt that, but whatever works for you," she said with a laugh. "Call me if you get lost." She finished her notes in Jack Bailey's chart and gave Carter a smile and a quick wave goodbye.

Carter watched her leave and as if not to be unkind, waved back even though she was well out of sight. He finished loading up the journals and looked around to make sure none of his belongings remained. He turned toward his grandfather.

"Well, I guess I'd better be heading out myself. I'll be

back tomorrow." He paused, as if waiting for some type of response, but knowing full well that none would be forthcoming. Reaching down, he touched his grandfather's hand.

"Have a good night, Grandaddy."

As he pulled in to Jessica's driveway a little after 6:00 p.m., Carter's GPS announced over the stereo system, 'You have arrived at your destination.'

"Yeah, with no thanks to you," he grouched. He had left in plenty of time knowing that he needed to allow a buffer in case he couldn't find her house, despite her directions and his electronic directional finder. Technology had failed him in this case as the GPS was firmly convinced it would require a ten mile jaunt all the way down to Morristown before circling around to reach Jessica's house from the west. Her directions indicated otherwise, so he deferred to her guidance and after a chorus of 'route recalculations' over the course of the past fifteen minutes, the unit attempted to claim credit for their success.

The house was a nondescript brick ranch; small, but well kept, probably built in the early 1960s. A hedge of tall blue spruce lined the right side of the yard as a buffer between Jessica's house and the property line next door, even though the neighbor lived several hundred yards away. The front of the house boasted an assortment of juniper, red tip, and hollies, all mature and well manicured. There was not a thing that seemed to be out of place or in need of maintenance.

He knocked on the storm door and peered past his reflection into the house. The main door was ajar and from somewhere inside he heard Jessica's voice call "Carter?" followed by a clank of pots and the thump of a cabinet.

"Yes, it's just me," he acknowledged, just in case she was expecting someone else.

"Come on in, make yourself at home. I'm just finishing the vegetables. I have some wine chilled if you'd like a glass."

"Great," he said as he let himself in and followed the sounds of activity until he found the kitchen. "I was going to bring a bottle along with me, but I remembered Tennessee doesn't sell wine in the grocery stores. I have no clue where I'd find a liquor store around here." Carter wasn't sure if the county was even wet.

Jessica laughed. "You're fine. I think I have everything we'll need. But thanks for the thought."

The inside of Jessica's house was not what Carter expected. Whereas homes of that age and style were accented with textured white walls, dark pine trim, and some variation of shag carpet, Jessica's home rivaled the style and décor of his Dunwoody condominium. Light hardwoods covered the floor throughout the living room and kitchen, accenting the blonde walls and white door and crown moldings. The furnishings were a collection of leather, wood, and fabrics that coordinated well with the accent pieces scattered around. The living area flowed into the kitchen with its light cabinetry, black granite countertops, and stainless appliances. A subzero refrigerator and Wolf stove caught his eye. He had priced those awhile back as upgrades to a kitchen that he hardly used. He had dismissed the idea since they wouldn't get a lot of use. But considering the rich, fragrant aromas that were filling the house, Jessica obviously knew what to do with them.

"Not what you were expecting?" Jessica asked as she moved a blend of vegetables and pasta into a white ceramic bowl.

"You've definitely given the place an updated look, considering its age. My compliments to your contractor. He did an excellent job."

Jessica stopped. "Why thank you, kind sir. I think I did

pretty well."

Carter turned and looked at her.

"YOU did all this?"

She responded with a slight shrug. "Yes...most of it, anyway, and not all at once. It's taken several years to complete. After Mom died and I went back to school, it helped break up the monotony and boredom a little. Turns out I had a knack for it and, after a few re-dos, I started to understand what worked and what didn't. Didn't touch the electrical and plumbing, though. I know my limits."

He nodded in acknowledgement, and a bit of envy, as the most he could do was ask around for a referral. His mind had served him well in making a living, but his hands were another matter entirely.

"I am definitely impressed," he said in earnest, moving toward the kitchen. "Did you say you had some wine?"

"Yes, in the refrigerator and the glasses are in the third cabinet down."

He poured a glass for himself and topped hers off, careful not to get in her way as she worked the various bowls and pots dotting the counter and stove, confirming that everything was progressing as it should. She pulled the ingredients for their first course from the refrigerator and deftly created a work of art as Carter watched. Mesclun greens, a blend of Dijon mustard and maple syrup, a tablespoon of chopped shallots, and teases of apples, topped with a sprinkling of aromatic feta. Her hands moved knowingly, combining each component with ease until the final result carried a visual, as well as potentially flavorful, promise.

With Jessica occupied, and Carter not wishing to be a hindrance to her efforts, he moved back into the living area to better appreciate the space she called home. The walls were carefully filled with shelving, lighting, and art in just the right balance to stay on the right side of couture and away from clutter. In the first set of shelving rested an assortment of what he assumed were family pictures; they ranged from antique sepia to full color. In the oldest picture, a face bearing a strong resemblance to Jessica stared back at him from the amber-toned paper and antique frame. Though the lighting of the room was comfortable, it was not conducive to detailed study. He took the frame from the shelf and moved to the window to catch the last rays of the sunset. A hint of recognition echoed in the back of his mind as he studied the picture.

"That's my grandmother," Jessica offered, stopping for a sip of wine as she put the finishing touches on the main course. "I favor her quite a bit."

He couldn't disagree.

"Except for the tone of the picture and the style of your hair, you could be twins."

He returned the picture to the shelf and scanned the remaining pictures of what he assumed were her mother, her father, friends, and who knew who else. Carter was pleased to notice, however, that there wasn't a particular man who showed up any more frequently than any other one. Always a good sign, he thought.

Next came a series of beautiful watercolor paintings of various mountain vistas and country scenes, from the bright burning colors of autumn to the lush green pictures of a mountain summer. Their beauty captivated him and in some ways reminded him of scenes from his childhood.

"I have to ask. Did you do these, too?" he asked, pointing to a rich portrait of fall color accentuated by an exotic wood frame.

Jessica pulled her attention from dinner to focus on his question. She looked at him, surprised.

"You give me way too much credit now," she remarked. "I'm a 'doer,' but not a very good 'creator'…unfortunately. It's a gift I would love to have."

"They're beautiful. All by the same artist?"

"Yes, his name is Jim Gray. He has several studios down in the Gatlinburg area. My mother and I went there each summer when I would come home for the Fourth of July holiday. We'd shop, walk around, eat, and whatever else we felt like doing. Our intent was just to be together. But his studio was always on the list. When I returned to D.C., I usually took a souvenir from his gallery home with me. That's how I started falling in love with Tennessee."

She took a deep breath and continued.

"She had just bought that one," she pointed to a scene of a mountain valley titled *I Look to the Hills*, "when a few weeks later she was diagnosed with cancer. It was the last one we bought together and, in some ways, that picture helped her through her darkest times. She'd call sometimes late at night, tired and sick with chemo, just wanting to talk about something, anything, other than medical stuff. Mom never complained, even during those times, but I could always tell when she was reaching her limit. She'd tell me, 'Jessie, you know where I am, dear?' and I'd always ask, 'Where, mama?' She'd say, 'I'm on that mountain, dear.... that mountain in that pretty picture looking at God's creation. It's so peaceful and serene...and so beautiful.' I truly think she went there in her mind when it got really bad."

She went quiet, reflecting on the friend and mother who had meant so much to her.

"I'm sorry you lost her so early. It sounds like you were very close." He paused. "Thank you for telling me that. I like knowing about the things that are important to you," he added earnestly.

She smiled. "You're welcome. And we were close. I'm not sad any more, but I do miss her still. I guess I always will." Jessica put a sprig of parsley garnish on the plate then made a gesture of presentation with her hand. "I think we're ready. I hope you're hungry."

The change in topic lifted the mood for both of them.

"Everything looks great, Jessica, and I'm starved. I apologize in advance if I make a pig of myself," Carter noted as he moved to the table.

They sat down to a meal of salad, wild mushroom ravioli with basil pesto sauce and an accompaniment of broiled asparagus, topped off with a dessert of coffee cheesecake with a cookie crumb crust. They talked about the simplest of topics as they ate; art, the challenges and pleasures of urban life, and the discoveries of common interests they held. At the conclusion of the meal, Carter lifted his wine glass and held it out in a silent toast to Jessica. She acknowledged his gesture, and after they drank, he lowered his glass and asked, "Is there anything you don't do incredibly well?"

She thought for a moment, then deliberately took her white cloth napkin and threw it across the table at him.

"Yes. Dishes."

"Fair enough," he laughed as he began clearing the dishes from the table.

She watched him move the glasses, plates, and bowls from the dining area into the kitchen and load the dishwasher. He wiped down the countertops and brought the last of the wine to top-off her glass.

Someone trained him well, she thought to herself as she went to sit down on the large downy couch in the living room.

Carter joined her, sliding in comfortably beside her.

"That was absolutely wonderful, Jessica," he said as he brought his glass to his lips. "You should start a restaurant some day." He was only half joking.

She beamed at the praise.

"Thanks, but I only cook for pleasure," then added, "and to see others happy. Besides, if I did it for money, it would lose most of its appeal."

He studied her quietly for a moment.

"So why did you leave your consulting firm?"

The first time he had asked about her past, it had made her uncomfortable. This time, however, she understood he was simply curious…and genuinely interested.

"When you asked me that last time, I had never truly put it all together. I didn't think about all the reasons." She looked at her wine glass, gently swirling what little liquid remained. "Two things happened at the same time and together they made me want to take my life in a different direction."

Carter was listening intently.

"Like a perfect storm?"

Jessica considered his statement. "No, not really. I would think of a perfect storm as when things converge for a bad result. This had a good outcome." She swallowed the last of her wine and placed her empty glass on the coffee table.

"What happened?"

Jessica sighed as she pulled memories out from that place she rarely ventured any more.

"I had been at the firm for several months, turning out good results, already bringing in new clients, etc., etc. I felt like I was doing exactly what the firm expected me to do, and more." She shifted and ended up closer to where Carter sat. "At least I thought I was. Brian, one of the partners, was encouraging me…supporting me. Always talking about the bright future I had."

"Then one day, a high dollar client decided he no longer wanted me on his account. This was after I had put my heart and soul into researching all possible avenues for him to execute the deal he wanted to make. Brian didn't back me at all."

"Gee, that's being supportive," Carter offered sarcastically.

"No kidding. It really made me angry." She hesitated

before adding, "Maybe I imagined it, but it also seemed as if he had a greater interest in me than just a professional one...and he was married."

Carter's face clouded. What had been a jab at a pathetic supervisor took on a more serious tone.

"OK, that's just plain wrong," he fumed. Carter would never consider taking advantage of someone who worked their tail off for him, and anyone who would made his blood boil. "Talk about the lowest of the low."

Jessica didn't say anything, but the feeling that she was good enough for the bedroom, but not good enough for the boardroom, had not diminished after all these years.

"Why did the client want you off his account?"

"Because I was a woman," she admitted with a hint of bitterness still in her voice. "He decided a man could do the job better. And since he was the one paying the bills..."

Carter just shook his head. "I didn't know it was still 1955. I'm sorry you had to experience that, Jessica."

She managed a half-smile.

"Thank you, Carter. I do appreciate that. I had some great clients and the consultants and analysts I worked with were just fantastic. I miss working with them, but...it was time to go."

Jessica continued. "All that happened at the same time Mom's prognosis became terminal and I decided I'd take a leave of absence to be with her. In my opinion, I wasn't leaving much behind. After she died, I understood how much she had needed me there and how much of a difference I had made to her in her last days. It had meaning...purpose. I was missing that in the life I was leading, even though it seemed like I had achieved 'success.' I decided I'd rather spend the rest of my days making a difference for people in their darkest hours than making people rich. So, that's how I ended up where I am today."

Carter didn't know what to say. Jessica had gone through

so much yet still stood so far above it all. She could have complained, griped, blamed others for everything, and lived with bitterness, but she simply didn't. Jessica Cooper just made her way forward, and he wondered if in the same situation if he would have fared nearly as well.

She broke into his thoughts.

"So, what did you read about Jack today? You seemed a little agitated when I saw you." Now it was her turn to satisfy her curiosity.

Carter leaned back into the couch, then sighed deeply.

"Today I read about him and my grandmother and how much he loved her. I always remembered them being so sweet together...like best friends for life. My grandfather sounded so devastated after his first wife left, but my grandmother's love seemed to give him a new purpose. He realized he had another chance and did everything he could to make it work."

He paused and shook his head.

"What?" Jessica asked, noting his expression.

"Remember when I mentioned that my grandfather had a habit of stopping sentences in mid-thought at the most inopportune time? He did it again at the end of the narrative noted with a '2.' It was like he was offering up an incredibly important point and then just forgot or didn't finish it for some reason."

"It would not be out of the question, considering it was the part he had recently written. He was well beyond reason when he moved into the hospice center. As it happened twice, do you think he did it intentionally?"

He sighed. "I don't know...I can't put my finger on it. What he wrote about himself and my grandmother was too brief. It ended so abruptly, so unexpectedly...he made their love sound so...well...simple."

He looked at Jessica.

"Is it really that simple?" he asked.

Jessica shrugged.

"I don't know...I hear it can be. I can't say I've ever experienced it." She studied his face. "What about love and Carter Lee...can I ask?"

The question caught him off guard. It was not his nature to open up about his own limitations, and his business persona had only reinforced that behavior over the years. Negotiation cannot be successful if the person across the table from you knows your weaknesses. But this was not a negotiation...and Jessica was not just someone across a table.

"Love and I aren't on a first name basis," he conceded. "I can't say I've had bad luck with it...that would mean I've had relationships that had some measure of love. I don't think I have." He looked away. "I could relate more to what my grandfather felt when his first wife left than what he felt for my grandmother..."

His response was something she easily understood.

"Why is that?"

Carter felt his anxiety level drop a little. "Work. Plain and simple. I believe it takes time and effort to make a relationship work and I just haven't felt like I've had the time to give a relationship a fair try," he said, sounding more like an apology than a statement in which he truly believed.

Jessica didn't say anything for a moment.

"That sounds too simple, Carter," she finally said. Though she had no history with this man on which to base her intuition, she felt he was holding something back.

He sat there, unable to meet her gaze. He knew she was right. He hated she was right, and it frightened him how easily she could look right through every layer of the façade he had carefully erected on this very private failure of his. Carter could lie, could bury his fears deeper than any place she could ever reach, but what would he gain from that?

His grandfather's words from the night before echoed through his mind: ...*it was because we didn't truly talk.*

She deserved to know the truth, and Carter knew the truth. He had known it all these years. As his failures in love mounted over the course of time, they only reinforced the potential reality of his fear coming to life. It was a very real reason to him and it didn't matter to him what anyone else thought about it—it was his fear and his fear alone. No one else ever had a reason to know...no one else until now.

He swallowed hard.

"When I was young, a friend let me borrow a movie about a guy who was drawn to a woman who lived in another time. He was so consumed with the need to be near her that he figured out how to travel back in time to be with her. He finally reached her and found what it was like to hold her and be loved by her." He paused before he continued. "And then he lost her. In one brief instant. It destroyed him and he died of a broken heart."

He looked at Jessica, his voice almost a whisper.

"I played that movie over and over. Watching him at the moment he realized he had lost her forever...I could feel my heart breaking along with his...a searing pain tearing through my chest. I had never experienced anything like it...and I've lived with the memory ever since. It was so real, it became so much a part of me. I wonder sometimes if I connected with it so strongly because that's what will happen to me. I'll find her, then I'll lose her, and I won't be able to get her back."

Tears began to fill her eyes. She put her hand over his, recognizing the tender honesty he was revealing to her. He was so open, so exposed, unlike anyone had ever been with her.

"You probably think I'm crazy. Dodging possums in the road...dreaming of a dying man...letting a movie from 20 years ago haunt me still..." He smiled weakly, having nothing left to hide and feeling completely vulnerable.

She touched the tip of his strong chin, pulling up his face so he could see her eyes.

"I think a lot of things about you," she said, searching his eyes, "crazy is not one of them." She took his face in her hands, gently cupping each cheek in her long slender fingers. Carter closed his eyes as she touched him, as if a lifetime of anticipation had just been realized. Her touch was so familiar to him, so wanted. He opened his eyes and saw mirrored in her eyes what he felt so strongly in his heart.

Jessica pulled his face closer, until she felt him respond. She leaned into him, meeting his kiss halfway, their lips touching tentatively at first, then giving way to the warmth and wetness of their tongues fulfilling the depth of their embrace. She broke off the kiss, pressing her cheek against his if only to absorb the intensity of the moment. His senses were keenly aware of everything now—the softness of her face against his, the feel of her hair, the lingering of her kiss on his lips, the very scent of her.

He hungered for her, but unlike all the women in his past, the very essence of her was all that would satisfy him. He slid his arm around her and firmly ran the tips of his fingers up and down her taught back, stopping in the small of her back to pull her into him as he kissed her again. She wrapped both arms around his neck and pulled him as tight as she could against her, filling his mouth with hers and taking all of him she could. He kissed her deeply, but gently, carefully balancing the desire that raged through him with the affection for her he harvested from the deepest parts of his heart. He slowly pushed her back against the cushions of the sofa, laying her down with his chest touching hers.

Their eyes embraced, each looking for resistance to the desire growing between them, but finding none. Fully and completely they needed each other and neither would stop until their souls intertwined. He began a small line of kisses from her mouth, up her cheek, then moving down her neck to the sensitive area where her neck and shoulder met. He kissed her there at first, then caressed her with his tongue as her body tensed in response. She was feeling desire she had never known with anyone before, as if a lifetime of comfortable intimacy had been born in one night. As he kissed her neck, she untucked his shirt and slid her hands underneath. He arched in response to her touch, his muscles tensing beneath her caress as he continued pleasuring her neck and shoulders.

Carter heard her shoes drop to the floor, then felt her legs move underneath him until he lay between them, her feet moving against his calves in slow rhythm with the unconscious motion of his hips. Need was coursing through every part of her body, and she desired him in the most instinctive of ways. She could feel the very beat of his heart against her chest crying out to hers. His breathing was as labored as her own, and she could not help but cry out softly when the touch of his body paired with hers in just the right way. Although their bodies desired more, their hearts knew better and each pulled back from the precipice of passion before passing the point of no return. They remained commingled in their embrace for the longest of times, their bodies still aching from the intensity of their kisses, touches, and caresses.

He lifted himself up just enough to slide between her and the back of the couch, then pulled her close against him again. She turned to look at him, her free hand taking his. His face was illuminated in the dim glow of the light from the candles on the mantle, his eyes catching their flicker every now and again. He pressed his face against hers as he pulled her close.

"Why do I feel like I've been missing you for a very long

time?" he quietly asked, a lifetime of questions lingering in his eyes.

Jessica closed her eyes and let his words wash over her. She waited before answering, though not for the lack of an answer.

"Yes…" she answered quietly. "It's as if some part of me I never knew existed has come alive. I don't have any words to describe it." She took his hand and placed it against her heart.

"Do you feel that?"

He felt the racing in her chest against his hand and nodded without saying anything.

"It's the only way I know to say it…"

Gently he took her hand and placed it against his chest.

"I know, Jessica…I know…"

They lay together quietly for several minutes, neither wanting the moment to ever end, to take them away from this.

"You know, I don't have to get up for work in the morning," Carter whispered in her ear.

She hesitated, but before she could answer, he continued.

"But you do, Jess." He smiled tenderly. "I'd better be going soon."

Jess. There was something so sweetly intimate about him calling her that, she thought.

"You're right. But I don't want you to go…not just yet…please…stay just a little while longer…"

Carter was not going to deny her anything at this point, much less a request that he also longed for. He smiled and kissed her softly before sliding up so she could lay her head on his chest and he could stroke her hair with his hand. It wasn't long before he felt her breathing become more even, the rise and fall of her chest more predictable. For a man who had spent most of his life alone, both emotionally and physically, her presence beside him was comfortably familiar. Their togetherness had only touched the very edges of intimacy, yet it had given him a feeling of contentment and peace that slowly pulled him into a peaceful and complete sleep.

Hours passed as night crept toward morning, their bodies still embraced as sleep had first found them. Just before dawn, Carter awoke, disoriented for a moment until he saw her lying beside him with her hand still resting over his heart. He slowly moved down so he could see her face, careful to not disturb her when he slid his arm from behind her back. It wouldn't be uncomfortable for him to stay longer, but he knew she had to get ready for work soon. He didn't want to disrupt her daily routine by being a welcome, yet unfamiliar, intrusion in her morning. Before he left, however, he just wanted to look at her, to see her for as long as he wanted without a reason or purpose.

Carter had had the pleasure of knowing many beautiful women over the years, largely on a professional basis, but occasionally on a more personal level. But in the back of his mind, there was always a face that lingered, one that encompassed every aspect of a woman's features he was drawn to. From the first time he had seen Jessica, the face that waited quietly in the corners of his mind had been given life, but he had not realized it until now. The curve of her face, the laugh of her eyes, and the subtle richness of her lips all touched him in ways even the most sensual of his past relationships never did. Carter desired Jessica beyond the realm of simple gratification. He was drawn to her, and for once, he wanted to give her everything he had to offer—no matter what the cost.

Carter gently placed his lips against her forehead in a quiet gesture of goodbye and moved slowly off the sofa. On the counter, he found a pen and a small pad of white paper on which he wrote a brief, but heartfelt, note that he placed in plain sight on the coffee table near where she lay. He wanted to ensure there was no question in her mind that he only left her side for an honest reason, and that the night before was just the beginning, not a one-time moment. To that, he was completely committed. The front door made barely a sound as he slipped out to head for home in the strange, gray, half-light of dawn.

FRIDAY

The house which I knew only as a dark, shadowy, cold domain a few days earlier now felt more like home. It was more familiar to me now, the memories from my past meshing with the experiences of the present to give it a familiarity that was uniquely its own. I felt at peace, surprisingly enough, and rested in a way that I couldn't recall in many years. Even though the evening with Jessica had abbreviated my sleep, I suffered no ill effects. In fact, I remained awake since returning from her house and was simply enjoying the lingering contentment of our time together.

I stepped out on the back porch to enjoy the quiet gift of the morning before the coming daylight took it away. The day was dawning clear and cool as the approaching autumn made its presence even more known. A blaze of scarlet burned across the tops of the mountains as the sun approached, the nighttime trying in vain to eek out every final moment of its existence. I had forgotten how the mountains speak in moments like these, reassuring all of us that darkness cannot hold out against the onslaught of light and glory.

Mountains ingrain themselves into the hearts of anyone who grew up within their shadow. When you return home after being away from their presence, you are reminded of the constant they represented in your life. They hold a familiarity for you, like the lines on the face of an old friend or the gentle approach of a lover. And they are part of even the simplest of memories. On summer nights in my youth, I would lay awake and listen to the rain on the oaks and maples outside my window....a mountain lullaby of sorts. The falling rain transformed the leafy arms of the trees into a thousand muted tympanis, and to that music I would drift off to sleep. Simple moments like that still remain with me, and my week here at the farm had given me a few more moments to treasure, to recall at some future time.

With my aunt returning the following week, the need for my stay in Sweet Branch was slipping away with each passing day. I wouldn't have more opportunities to simply sit and be, and I felt the need to drink in whatever little moments like this I could. I had been sitting quietly by myself when around the corner came Brown Dog, ready to renew our relationship in her quiet, peaceful way. She moved up beside me, cuddling up against my side as if signaling for me to wrap my arm around her. I was happy to comply, her silent companionship a peaceful complement to the memory the morning was becoming. We were comfortable, she and I, even though our relationship consisted of but a few head rubs and private conversations over the course of the past few mornings.

It doesn't make sense to some, but anyone who has ever had a dog knows they have the enviable gift of complete and total acceptance, which makes anyone their new best friend in no time at all. I ran my hand across the soft fur of her belly and leaned my head against hers, getting an acknowledging nudge of affection in return. We sat that way for several minutes, requiring nothing of each other except companionship. Finally, she turned towards me and nuzzled my cheek with her wet nose as if to say goodbye, then ambled away to a destination that only she knew.

"Goodbye, Brown Dog," I softly called after her, as the thought of potentially getting a dog of my own ran across my mind. Last week, definitely not. This week, maybe it was something to put on the list.

I had nothing in the house worth eating, and I was incredibly hungry. The small diner where I had first eaten upon arriving in town had advertised a full country breakfast—served any time—and this seemed as good an 'anytime,' and day, as any other. I showered, shaved, cleaned up, and even borrowed one of my grandfather's flannel shirts to accompany my attire of jeans and boots. Looking in the mirror, I looked more like a local than an outsider, and felt a hint of pleasure as a result. I was starting to see why Jessica decided to call Sweet Branch home.

While I was ready to satisfy my hunger, I was also looking forward to seeing Jessica again. Last night had been so good, and though we had spent most of the night together, nothing had occurred that would cause even a hint of regret this morning. This morning after held no pain—only promise. As I reached for the door, I happened to notice my Blackberry lying on the stand next to the doorway. I stared at it for a moment, then dismissed it as I left the house, without even picking it up.

Connie Leonard felt awful. Johnny, her youngest, had spent the better part of the night either throwing up or crying, whichever his body required or permitted, and he had not calmed down until just before daylight. Her husband, being the worthless slob of underpaid laziness he was, had not lifted a finger to help, despite having no particular place to go today. Connie had to handle everything and her head did not touch her pillow the entire night. As a result, she was beyond exhausted, inching closer to delirium, the end of the day seemingly eons away. Jack Bailey was first on her rounds today and, luckily, it was just a shave and a change of linens. She was thankful for even one easy patient today.

She was just putting the razor to his face when Carter Lee broke into her exhausted trance.

"Could...I...help you do that?" he asked somewhat tentatively. "I'm not much good with bed linens, but I can lend a hand shaving." Ever since she had asked him yesterday, Carter had felt a hint of guilt about how he had reacted, as if caring for his grandfather was something beneath him. It wasn't, and with everything he had learned about him over the past few days, Carter found himself wanting to give something of himself to his grandfather. Maybe this wasn't the most demonstrative act of compassion the world had ever known, but for Carter, the symbolism was beyond anything he would have been capable of when he first arrived. His grandfather would understand if he were able.

"Sure thing," Connie replied, more than glad to mark one obligation off her list so early in the day. It meant she was that much closer to her lunch break, when she could take a quick nap in the privacy of her car and try to salvage what remained of the day.

"Here's the razor, a little soap, and you can use this basin to wash the razor out." She handed her supplies over quickly, just in case he was regretting his offer, and practically ran out the door without looking back.

Jessica had just finished her first rounds and was walking toward Jack Bailey's room at a fairly steady pace. She had been thinking of Carter all morning and wanted to see if he had arrived yet. She had discovered his note, just as he intended, and she was moved by his thoughtfulness in making sure she knew why he had left. It was welcome, but certainly not necessary. Never in her life had she felt so complete in the arms of a man. Though logic would advise caution with one she had known for such a short time, her heart simply didn't care and found ample reason to reaffirm all was good in the world, especially the world with Carter Lee.

She approached Jack's room, and as she did, she caught a glimpse of Carter standing beside Jack's bed holding something near Jack's face. It took a moment for her to see what he was doing, but once she did, Jessica was deeply touched by the scene she witnessed. Yet again, he was showing her, without consciously trying to, how wrong she had been about him the first time they met. Jessica wasn't going to interrupt this moment between a grandfather and grandson, especially with so few opportunities for such times remaining. She watched for just a few minutes longer, then slowly turned and walked away, the memory of the moment forever burned into her heart.

Carter finished rinsing the razor in the basin and placed it on the bedside table. With the hand towel he had tossed over his shoulder, he gently wiped away any remaining soap from his grandfather's face, then dried the razor completely in case it was to be used again the next day. He saw a small comb on the bedside table so he took the opportunity to smooth his grandfather's hair into a more presentable state. Stepping back, he critiqued his work and came away reasonably satisfied with the job he had done. It was not a perfect shave by any means, but he had done it for his grandfather. And that's what mattered most to him.

It was already 9:30 and he had yet to see Jessica, which was odd. He'd have to go track her down if he didn't see her within the next half hour, just to make sure she had made it into work. He had not considered it at the time, but his leaving her on the couch may have caused her to miss her alarm and oversleep, which was not the way he wanted last night to end.

Carter had just finished putting the shaving supplies

back into the bathroom when Jessica strolled into the room, unable to wait any longer to see him. She already had a smile on her face, which immediately wiped away any hint of worry Carter had about how she was feeling about last night—and he was relieved she had not overslept.

"The last thing I wanted to do this morning was to leave you...I hope you know that," Carter blurted out, wanting to make that point abundantly clear.

She grinned.

"I do. I really do. You could have stayed...it would have been all right." She paused, hesitant to say anything about a next time. "I found your note...it was so sweet of you to make sure that I understood why you left..."

"I didn't want there to be any question. It was a wonderful night for me, I just want you to feel that way, too."

"I do, Carter. I wouldn't have changed a thing."

They moved to embrace and lingered in each other's arms before resuming their proper roles of caregiver and concerned family member.

"I have to teach a class from 10 until 4 today so I won't be around much," she told him, noticing his attire for the first time. "Well, hey, bubba. Aren't we fitting in with the natives?" She gave a carefree laugh, then sized him up. "You pull off the look rather well."

"Hey, thanks," he said, shifting from one foot to the other. He couldn't recall the last time a woman had complimented the way he looked. "I think I could get used to it."

"I can't say as I blame you. You should consider it on a full-time basis," she said with a wink. "I'll drop by when I'm done." She kissed his check, lingering for just a moment, then left.

Carter sat down in the chair and began his now-daily ritual of poring through the remaining journals. Yesterday had taken him through the bulk of his grandfather's life, up until the time his grandmother had passed away a few years ago. There were still a few journals to read, which surprised him, considering his grandfather's advancing age and their fully-handwritten nature. It was hard enough for him to handwrite anything longer than two or three pages; the computer had spoiled, or ruined, him in that respect. But his grandfather, in his advanced stage and likely dealing with a touch of arthritis, had continued to churn out written words upon the page year over year. As he had for the past few days, Carter continued the journey through his grandfather's life, entering the twilight of Jack Bailey's time on Earth.

The final journals were just as vibrant and rich as any his grandfather had written in his life. Observations of his current failing state, memories of times past, and hope for the future that he would probably never see filled the pages, written as if his grandfather was speaking directly to him in one final, documented goodbye. Every now and then the tone would reach out into the darkness of depression and futility, questioning whether continued life was a blessing or a curse. He was probably lonely by now, struggling with the finality of life, Carter thought. But his grandfather persevered, never letting the dark times linger too long, fighting back with a thought or a memory from the past that somehow showed that it had all been worth it—that everything had been worth doing—and that he was just glad to be here.

Carter closed the last journal with a pang of remorse. With the exception of what lay within the pages of the small binder, his grandfather had nothing left to say. Their time together was now done and the suddenness of it caught Carter off guard. Up until now, he had not considered that this moment would come. The endless piles of journals had made pondering this moment frivolous, but now the desk was bare and the emptiness of that truth weighed upon

Carter's heart. It was with humble appreciation that he pulled the binder with the yellow note pages from his backpack and turned to the final section...the final conversation they would have together...narrative #3. He began to read.

There is an old saying that love is blind. As I've always understood it, it means that no matter what faults, issues, or warts that someone whom you love has, you won't care because you are so overcome by love. Nothing else matters but being near them. I believe love is blind, but in a much different way. It happened when I was a young man.

Friends are a curious enigma. Some are integral parts of the most wonderful memories you create. Others cause you more grief than pleasure, mainly because they are more acquaintances than friends, but for whatever reason, we've given them a prime position in our lives. Then you have the pinnacle—those non-blood related individuals with whom you feel a kinship greater than family.

Families aren't necessarily biological. It may sound funny, but people you aren't related to can take care of you and love you just as well as, and sometimes better than, your blood kin. Or maybe teach you something that you didn't know about the intimacies of being human. Or show you how to love. Annie was that type of person.

From the time we were young, Annie was always a part of my life. Whether it was playing in a creek on a sweltering hot July day, sledding down a hill in the middle of winter, or exploring the trails and paths that dotted our area on an autumn afternoon, we were usually doing it together. When boys and girls are young, they rarely notice the differences of gender. They are simply drawn to those kindred spirits who can 'whoop' when it feels good, can get lost for hours in play, and can understand the intricacies of eating a jelly sandwich while balancing on a fence post; all the basic requirements of youth.

As Annie and I matured, our conversations followed; replacing the child-like curiosity about bugs and flowers with questions about the world and what the future held. We remained partners on this journey of life, celebrating the highs, commiserating on the lows, and even laughing at life, at our peculiar circumstances, at ourselves—with pure, simple joy.

One spring afternoon I decided it was time to try smoking like the other men in my family, and I tried to pull Annie into my experiment. She refused to be party to my ignorance, berating me for even considering such a thing. Undaunted, I stole tobacco and wrapping papers from my father's coat and snuck out to the outhouse where I was certain I would not be disturbed. After rolling a solid cigarette just like my father, and lighting it like one who had smoked for years, I tried to enjoy this newfound pleasure. Halfway through, I questioned why anyone enjoyed the burning sensation in their throat or the vile smell in their nostrils. Toward the end, I had pretty much decided that this was not for me, and if I could close out this entire experience without anyone—namely my father—noticing, I would have done well. It made no sense to be disciplined for something that I had no intention of ever doing again.

I looked out through the slats of the outhouse and didn't see a soul in the yard. A sigh of tobacco-scented relief left my lungs as I realized I was going to get away with this nightmarish experiment. Before I opened the door, I had to get rid of the cigarette remains and, since no one I knew slopped around the outhouse hole, it seemed to be the right place to put it.

I was a decent student in school, but not a great one. I was especially not great in science. If I HAD been great in science, I would have learned that human waste can produce methane gas. I would have also learned that methane gas is flammable, and that a huge buildup of methane gas is extremely flammable. I would have topped off my education by understanding that when a flammable object meets an ignition source like...oh...a burning cigarette, combustion can occur. Which is what happened to me...and the outhouse.

One can imagine the ridicule and humiliation that comes from being the one in a small community who blew himself up sitting in the outhouse. My physical injuries were minor; some singed hair and a red bottom (from my father, not from the fireball). But my pride took a terrible hit. Annie, though, never rubbed it in, never said 'I told you so.' She just accepted me for who I was and how stupidly pigheaded I could be.

The summer I turned 18 we developed a simple ritual, quite by accident. Late one Friday afternoon in June, I was working the upper fields of our farm where we planted acres and acres of corn. From this vantage point, one could see for miles in all directions with only the rustle of the oaks and maples disturbing the silence. I stopped my weeding to rest and just happened to look down the ridge and saw Annie coming up the trail with a burlap bag. She now worked at Mr. Pennington's mill, one of the few places in our area that a young woman just learning skills could find work at a decent wage.

We didn't get to spend as much time together as we used to. The most we did these days was just wave in passing as she headed home for the night and I was finishing up in the fields. Today, though, was different. When she reached the top of the hill where I stood, Annie opened up the burlap sack and pulled out two bottles of ice cold Coca-Cola, two rolls, some cheese, and two apples. Over those two bottles of Coke and our simple meal, we made up for the time that adulthood was taking away from us, allowing ourselves for just an instant to be carefree and hopeful again. We sat on that ridge together for hours until the summer sun finally surrendered to the Tennessee night.

From that point through the end of the summer, we shared two bottles of Coke, a simple meal of some sort, and whatever else we felt every Friday evening. Some days we talked about her work at the mill and how she longed to do something different some day. Some days we talked about the good and the bad of staying where we were, that a familiar life had its merits and pitfalls. Other times we simply shared silent company—often more comforting than any words of advice. We could do anything or nothing and have the best time.

We were changing individually as we inched toward adulthood, but our relationship did not have to change. We had something very special together and no matter what life would throw at us, it seemed like we would always be Jack and Annie. And that was good, because the coming autumn would bring a change for me. I would be leaving to go to college, an opportunity I had longed for since I was twelve. We talked about it quite a bit over that summer. What I would see, what I would do....when I would come home again. We promised to write and stay connected because we were friends, and though we never said it, we were also seeing each other in a different way. The way that men and women see each other that is pure, simple, and honest. The way that includes your whole heart.

As the time to leave approached, I became nervous...nervous about leaving, nervous about what it would be like, nervous about the unknown. It bothered and haunted me, causing me to be distant from everyone, including Annie. The reality that I would be away from the security of my home for a long period of time was starting to sink in. I felt apprehensive, almost scared, with each passing day and I could not think of anything else. This new chapter in my life would teach me many things about being on my own and making my own way, and I knew it was something I must do if I wanted a better future. But before this new chapter would even begin, I would learn that you can do something in an instant that will give you heartache for life. That lesson came on the day I left for college.

The air on that day was touched with the caress of the coming autumn. I stood on the platform watching other young men and their families making indiscriminate conversation until the moment of parting came. A shiver ran through my body, not from the weather as much as from the twinge of homesickness already building in my belly. Going off to school had been a dream of mine, like waiting for my birthday party so I could be the guest of honor. But, unlike birthdays, this was not a moment I was enjoying. All the apprehension I had felt about leaving home was coming to life in this moment, and I was already questioning whether this was something I really wanted to do. Maybe I could just stay here, I thought. But that wasn't the best option for me…and I knew it. This was something I had to do.

In the distance, a puff of smoke slowly rose from the horizon, growing larger with each moment. The tension on the platform escalated with the approaching train, and slowly the inevitable moment arrived. I looked around, breathing in the beauty of the area I had so often taken for granted. I looked at my mother standing there, smiling the smile that every man knows when he leaves home for the final time as a child. It says, `You are a part of my life I swore I would never release, but now I know that the world will not let me keep that promise. I will smile until the train is far down the tracks, until you can no longer see my face or the tears behind my eyes. But once gone from sight, I will weep for the sweetest days of my life that I know will never be mine again. You have been my greatest joy, my son, and I will not give up my right to miss you.'

I hugged her goodbye and boarded the train that now sat at the station, its brakes hissing steam in the cool mountain air. The train filled quickly, as our small town was but a brief stop on the way to Virginia. As the train began to lurch forward, I saw Annie just across the way, running to the station. In her arms she carried a burlap bag, and on her face a look of sadness and hurt. She stopped, and out from the bag came two bottles of Coke tied together with a red ribbon, the most symbolic gift of us, ready for me to take.

But I couldn't. It was too late. The train was too far gone. I felt my heart break as I watched this beautiful girl standing there, staring after me as I disappeared into the distance. At that moment I realized what I had done…or not done…to my beloved Annie. I had not told her my departure date had moved up one *day. I had simply forgotten. She did not know I was leaving today...and who knows what she was thinking.*

It wasn't on purpose. Annie had become so ingrained in my life that I couldn't imagine her not knowing everything about and within me. But I had failed her and in doing so, hurt her more deeply than anything I could have done. Seeing her standing there with that pain on her face, knowing that she had cared enough for me to give me something so dear and special to us...and that I had let her down...let us down...was more than I could bear.

One of the curses of that day and age was that communication was very, very slow. Painfully slow. They say that true friendship continues to grow, even over the longest distance, and that the same goes for true love. But pain also grows over distances, especially when you cannot communicate with the one you've hurt, but care about so much. You replay the scenes over and over in your mind, reliving the pain time after excruciating time. The next day I wrote a letter to Annie trying to explain that it was all a mistake, that I had been overcome by going away to school and that I had simply forgotten. I told her I missed her, that she meant more to me than anyone, and she was the one person in the world I would never want to hurt. But explanations like that often put us deeper into a hole and, though we know the truth, the truth somehow gets lost in the written word and never makes the point we intended it to.

I didn't tell her the things I should have, either...like each night before I fell asleep, it was her face I saw. That whenever I gazed up at the moon through my bedroom window in the dead of night, I wondered if maybe she was, too. That sometimes, for no apparent reason, I imagined I felt the softness of her hair against my face. And that I loved her...I was just blind and didn't know it until I saw her standing there as the train pulled away. Why I did not tell her the depth of my feelings when I had the chance is a mystery that haunts me to this day...and always will.

Two months later, I did receive a response from Annie. It was polite, courteous, and in a way sounded like our conversations on the hill about the events of the week. Only toward the end did she acknowledge what had happened and give me any indication of how badly it had affected us. She told me that no matter how good a friend is, they're going to hurt you every once in awhile, and you must forgive them for that. And she forgave me. It was a simple acknowledgement, but it confirmed what I already feared: I had hurt her deeply.

Things never were quite the same after that. Annie and I would correspond, but soon the letters became further and further apart, their content more general with each passing note. Finally, she wrote to tell me she had met a nice man from the Midwest and that he had plans for their future that included their moving away from Sweet Branch. She wanted me to hear that from her and hoped I would understand...and be happy for her.

We lost touch for decades after that. Though we were distant in time, 'we' were still a large part of who I was and not a day went by that I did not think of her...wondering what her life might be like. In a corner of my heart, I held on to the hope that maybe one day I could see her one more time, to tell her all the thoughts and feelings that the young man from the mountains of east Tennessee should have told her long ago...but didn't. I would not forget this time, and in my hands would be two bottles of ice cold Coke tied with a red ribbon.

One afternoon, years ago, I was visiting with friends when they asked, 'Wasn't it sad what happened to Annie?'

'What happened to Annie,' I asked quietly, feeling my chest tighten.

'An aggressive form of non-Hodgkin's lymphoma,' I was told. It was in an advanced stage when they found it so there wasn't much anyone could do. She died two months after being diagnosed. They said it was such a shame, as she always talked about returning to our hometown, just one more time, while she still could. If the cancer had not been so fast moving, she may have been able to make the trip now that she knew her time was short. But there was just no way. She got too sick too quickly. 'Such a

shame,' they said. They continued on with their sharing of other news, and not so newsworthy, items but my interest in the conversation stopped the moment they broke my heart.

Annie. My sweet Annie. Gone. Forever. It just could not be. All the thoughts of what we had shared, the time spent reliving the painful moment I realized I had hurt her so deeply, and the longing for even the slightest communication from Annie over the past decades came tumbling together in a painful, twisted way.

It's unreasonable to even feel this strongly about it, I told myself, but logic and reason don't amount to much at times like this. There was nothing else I could do, however, nothing more I could hope for at this point. All I could do was say goodbye.

That night, I bound up my last gift for Annie in my coat, crept out the back door, and took a walk underneath the crescent moon to a little knoll just at the edge of the pasture. From my coat I took two ice-cold bottles of Coke, tied with a red ribbon, and gently placed them on the ground...returning a favor from so long ago. A last ritual before the 'we' I cherished so much said goodbye; only this time, I was the one staying behind while she was on the journey to a far away place that I could not go...not yet, anyway.

I wanted her to know that I never forgot that image of her or how much it meant to me that she did what she did. I felt tears well up in my eyes as I accepted there would never be another chance in this lifetime to let Annie know how much she meant to me. Though I married a wonderful woman and had been blessed with beautiful children and grandchildren to love, a part of me still belonged to her. I had held onto the most fragile hope that somehow, someway, the day would come when I could set everything right and have the chance to see what she and I could truly become. That hope, and a part of me, died with Annie.

I looked up at the stars for the longest time, scanning the breadth of God's universe, but looking for nothing in particular. Maybe Annie looked down that night and saw me sitting there, Cokes in hand, and understood what I was trying to say. Or *maybe she was there with me, right beside me, head on my shoulder staring out across the valley like we used to do. Maybe she even used the whisper of the wind and the gentle force of the breeze to touch my face just one more time to say, "It's OK Jack...I know you loved me...and I loved you, too." I will never know...not in this lifetime at least...but an old man can dream. I do know that my life without Annie would not have been the same...that I would not have changed anything about the time we spent together, except to make it longer...and that things really do go better with an ice-cold Coke.*

Goodbye, Annie. I love you...probably more than you will ever know. I know I was not perfect, but I loved you in the best way I knew how. I will still miss you every day—for the rest of my days.

Carter was stunned. It's not his grandmother, but some other woman, who had his grandfather's heart all these years. He looked at the comatose figure lying in the bed beside him. Without saying a word, his grandfather had completely shattered the perception he had of his family's idealistic existence, especially that of its patriarch. Carter slowly laid the binder down on his lap and blindly stared ahead.

What in the world do I do with this information? He could tell Jessica, but she didn't have the frame of reference to understand its significance. All she knew about his family she had gained from him. Tell his mother or his aunt? It would kill them. The family had struggled enough with the idea that Jack was married before. To know there was another woman who had held a portion of his heart for all these years would be devastating, especially to his mother and the relationship she still treasured with her father. It appeared to Carter that this new piece of information was his to grapple with, and to grapple with alone.

He leaned back against the chair and closed his eyes. A

pounding ache was building behind his eyes and it would only get worse if he let himself get too worked up over this latest development in the saga of Jack Bailey. He tried to block out all the sound and light that surrounded him and relax for a few minutes in the hope that the pain would go away.

Maybe some quiet time would help, he thought. The effect of his late evening with Jessica and the volume of reading he'd completed over the course of the afternoon conspired to lull Carter into a comfortable, drowsy state. It wasn't long before he was drifting through the stages of sleep in the quiet room that was warming quickly from the rays of the afternoon sun.

It wasn't clear how much time had passed before he was conscious of another presence in the room. Carter pulled himself from the grip of sleep with a start and, when his vision had cleared, his eyes came to rest on the figure of a man sitting at the foot of his grandfather's bed.

The man was familiar, but it took a second before Carter realized why he felt a cold chill washing over him. The man was his grandfather.

Carter looked at the bed where his grandfather still lay, then back to the embodiment of Jack Bailey smiling at him from only a few feet away.

"Hello, Carter," the man said.

Carter didn't begin to know what to say. He just stared at the man as his body subtly pulled into a defensive posture.

"I hope I didn't startle you," the man continued, speaking in a manner that mirrored his relaxed stance. "It wasn't my intent if I did."

"That would be somewhat of an understatement," Carter said, finally finding his voice after his breathing resumed.

"You flat scared the hell out of me. And if you don't mind me saying so, you still are."

The moment was surreal. Carter became mindful that his hands were clamped solidly onto the chair, as if to steady him against whatever force might try to take him away.

His grandfather laughed warmly, his steel blue eyes relaying the contentment of a man at peace.

"You'll have to forgive me, Carter. I'm somewhat new to all this. It's not anything I've ever experienced before."

Before he could even ask another question, Jack stood up and motioned for Carter to follow him. He moved towards the door and was out into the hallway when he realized Carter was still embedded in the chair. Jack stopped, turned, and looked at him.

"Carter. Please." he gently requested.

Carter didn't know what else to do. He slowly arose from the chair and, with a passing glance at the form still laying in the bed, followed his grandfather toward the hallway.

His next step should have taken him to a long hallway with tight nap carpet, textured wall covering, and a bath of bright fluorescent lighting. Instead, he found himself on the front porch of a beautiful farmhouse, freshly painted and bathed in the scent of jasmine, roses, and honeysuckle. It was his grandfather's house, only much more inviting and welcoming than when he had left it this morning.

"Have you ever seen anything so beautiful," Jack exclaimed, raising his arms as if to embrace all of God's creation in one emphatic clutch. "I have missed this old place so much...so many good memories."

The aesthetics of the country scene were the least of Carter's concerns at the moment. He was still struggling with how in the world he ended up where he was.

As if reading Carter's thoughts, Jack laughed and made his way over to a gleaming white rattan love seat facing out toward the yard. He sat down and, with a sigh of satisfaction, leaned back with his hands on the back of his head.

"Go ahead, Carter. Take a rest."

Standing in what was either an incredibly detailed dream or a portal to another time, Carter struggled to make sense of what was happening. He was with a man who should be lying in a bed in a hospice center. Actually, at last check, he seemingly WAS still lying in a bed in a hospice center, yet here he was in living form. The location was familiar...but wasn't, and his companion mirrored the contradiction. From Carter's perspective, everything was unfamiliar, but he appeared to be the only one who felt this way. He was the stranger in a strange land.

He cautiously walked over to a wooden rocker and eased into it as the slat boards creaked a welcome. Carter Lee was not at all at ease.

"You've done quite a bit of reading these past few days, haven't you?"

Carter winced at the question, aggravating his already tense state.

"Yes...yes I have." The hesitancy in his voice belied the embarrassment he felt at his obvious invasion of his grandfather's private words.

"It's OK, Carter. It really is. I'm actually glad you had a chance to read my writings." Jack had moved to the edge of his seat. "What did you think?" he asked, seemingly eager to know Carter's thoughts.

Carter took the conversation to another place instead.

"What's happening here? I'm not sure if I'm dreaming or if this is real...?" His words trailed off.

Jack moved back in his seat, a hint of disappointment in his eyes.

"I don't know if it's real or not Carter. You'll have to decide that for yourself. There are some things I don't understand myself." He looked out into the distance. "You may just have to trust me on this one."

At that moment, they heard a bark, immediately followed by Brown Dog bounding around the corner.

"Patch!!! Hi, sweet girl! What are you doing here?" Jack exclaimed. The dog who had befriended Carter bounded onto the porch and raced to Jack's outstretched hand. Though she was staid and quiet each time Carter had seen her, she had regressed into an excitable ball of puppy-like joy, jumping up into Jack's lap and licking his face as he rubbed her stomach.

"I have missed you so much, Patch! I didn't think I would ever see you again." Now Jack was as excited as Patch was, leaving Carter even more confused.

"You know her?"

Jack raised his eyebrows in surprise.

"Oh, yes. This is Patch. She was my buddy for nearly fourteen years, from when I graduated college. Got her when she was a puppy from old man Grainger when his bird dog got pregnant from a stray. He was going to get rid of the whole litter, but I saved her just in time. I didn't know how lucky I was to get her." He stopped and put his face against hers, then looked at Carter quizzically. "You've met?"

Carter remembered the old photograph of the dog on his grandfather's desk with the same name on the back...and the year noted as 1948.

"Yes, as a matter of fact. We've been spending mornings together, although she hasn't been nearly this excited to see me." Carter smiled in spite of himself. He wasn't going to ask about the picture on the desk; he wasn't sure he wanted to know.

"I missed her so much when she died. She passed when I was about your age, I guess. I felt like I had lost my best friend," Jack said as he wrapped both arms around Patch as if she was an overstuffed teddy bear.

"I learned a lot," Carter offered quietly after a few minutes of respecting their simple reunion.

Jack furrowed his brow and said nothing.

"About you...your journals."

Jack smiled at him, letting Patch lay down on the seat beside him so he could make up for all the years of lost belly rubs.

"I hope you don't mind," Carter repeated, not so much for his grandfather's reconfirmation, but his own need to get past his discomfort about everything he now knew. "I just stumbled on them and..."

"Like I said, Carter, it's OK", Jack interrupted. "I never understood my need to record everything like I did. It just became a habit and, I have to admit, I wondered from time-to-time if it was just an exercise in futility. My life wasn't that interesting in most ways."

"Well, Annie was certainly a surprise...," Carter blurted out. "Did grandmother know?" Carter's initial uneasiness had been replaced by a demanding curiosity to understand something that could change the very essence of how he viewed his family's patriarch.

Jack looked away into the distance again.

"It's complicated, Carter."

"Complicated? That's not an answer." Carter felt his agitation rising.

"From what I've read, it seems like you were living a lie," Carter brazenly put forth. His own defiance surprised him. For years, and especially in the past few days, he had felt left out and hurt by the lack of relationship between himself and a man that so many held in such high esteem. If what he inferred was anywhere near true, he had worried about and endured it all for nothing.

What would normally invoke a defensive response in any man, much less one being directly confronted by his own grandson, instead brought a tone of conciliation from the man across the porch.

"I know what it looks like, Carter. I can understand your being upset. But things are not always as they appear."

Carter caught his emotions before they raised to another level entirely and deferred to the professional demeanor he had cultivated over the years.

"Explain it to me, then." He waited.

Jack stood up and, followed by Patch, made his way to the seat beside Carter. He took a deep breath.

"Carter, don't misunderstand. I loved your grandmother very much. But there are different kinds of love. What I had with your grandmother was very loving, very comfortable…very special. But if I'm true to my heart, what I felt for Annie went beyond anything I ever experienced. She touched me in a way no one else ever did, in a way I didn't realize. I was too young to recognize it and, in many ways, too foolish. Every once in awhile there is that person whose heart aligns with yours, whose soul is the perfect complement to who you are, to what's inside of you. It simply can't be duplicated." He stopped, searching for the right words.

"Once you've realized you've missed it, it's a horrible, empty pain that you never quite recover from…and you never forget."

The words hung in the air while Carter absorbed them. He couldn't relate, on any level, to someone that could affect you so deeply that it haunted you for the rest of your days. He questioned how could anyone love and carry on a life with another knowing the specter of love's regret was hanging in the shadows.

The look on Carter's face told Jack Bailey everything he needed to know.

"You simply don't understand…do you?"

His question was met with the silence of a man who had no answer.

"Come with me, Carter. You need to experience something."

Jack reached out and touched his grandson's arm and instantly Carter found himself on what seemed to be a platform, elevated along a railroad track in a small mountain town. It was a brisk, early fall day with a deep blue morning sky accentuating the changing colors of the mountain tops. The rich smell of a wood fire from somewhere unseen filled the air and, every now and then, a pristine antique car drove by on the dirt-swept road that paralleled the railroad tracks. A few steps away stood a young man of about 18 years talking to a woman with tears in her eyes. In the distance echoed the mournful cry of a steam locomotive, growing louder as it approached the platform.

The young man and the older woman shared words that Carter could not discern, eventually resulting in a long embrace that ended just before the train pulled to a stop. She pulled him close one more time, then released him as he reached down to pick up a suitcase and coat that rested at his feet. As the man entered the train car, Carter and his grandfather drifted with him, seemingly invisible to any and all around them. Up into the baggage shelf went the young man's suitcase, followed by his coat, and he deposited himself on the leather covered bench seat directly underneath. From somewhere down the platform a voice informed, 'All aboard. Next stop, Bristol, Virginia,' although the few passengers awaiting the train at this stop had long ago boarded.

Carter felt the lurch of the train pull their car in a long sequence of momentum as the journey began. As the train began to move, Carter caught the image of a young girl in a white dress and blue sweater moving along the road just ahead of the platform. Her pace immediately quickened as she realized the train was moving forward, her hands pulled up to her chest as she protected whatever package she was carrying. The young man caught sight of her at the very same moment as Carter and shot up out of his seat, pressing his hands against the window. The young woman's eyes locked onto him and reversed her direction to begin running with the train, as if her discovery could help her catch up with the combination of steel and steam that was slowly gaining speed. The young man mouthed something Carter could not hear at the same time the young woman realized the futility of her goal, and slowly came to a stop. Without the motion of her body, it became clear what she carried in her hands: two bottles of a dark liquid, bound with a red ribbon. Carter then realized what he was experiencing...and who he was seeing.

His grandfather suddenly took Carter's hand and placed it on the shoulder of the young man staring out the window. A rush of pain burned through Carter's entire body, meeting in the very center of his chest. His jaw tightened and a panic unlike any he had ever experienced began building in his stomach. His vision tunneled to the young girl on the dirt road who was quickly fading from view as the great locomotive made its way forward. It took everything Carter had to not burst into tears, the emotions pressing against every seam of self-control he possessed. A dam was breaking, his limit was fast approaching, and he felt as if he would explode.

And then it stopped.

He found himself returned to the front porch of his grandfather's house, the serenity of the scene uninterrupted by the events of the past few moments. Carter stared at the gray porch floor, struggling to bring his heaving chest into a more normal rhythm. He felt an intense sense of lingering sadness from what he had just experienced and could not look at his grandfather until he regained some semblance of composure.

Finally Carter found his voice.

"Why did you do that to me..."

Jack did not speak for several minutes. Eventually he looked at his grandson with a mix of regret and purpose echoing in his eyes. It pained him to inflict the pain he had experienced so long ago on one of his own, but he had felt he had no other option.

"Carter, something is happening to you that I'm so afraid you will miss. That's why I not only wanted you to know what I experienced, but to experience it yourself...to feel it and know. To understand how it felt to lose the one you love. You can gain love, you can lose love, but you only have one chance with THE love. I missed mine...I don't want you to miss yours...with Jessica."

"How do you even know that she and I are—"

"It's because everything I experienced before your mother was conceived is a part of you. In the very makeup of who you are. You are connected to things that meant everything to me. You may not know why you have a familiar feeling or a memory or a thought about something new; some call it déjà vu, but you are simply living a recollection of mine or one of our ancestors from long ago. It's why you loved your grandmother the way you did...because she was special to me and your mother. It's the reason you feel and need the mountains in your life like you do...yet have forgotten...because I drew such strength from them."

He paused.

"And it's why you love Jessica like you do...because I loved her grandmother so much. And it's why she feels the way she does about you...because her grandmother loved me the same way. It's a part of who you and Jessica are...because of me and Annie..."

"You mean the girl was—"

"Yes, Carter. Annie was Jessica's grandmother...just as you are my grandson."

The face in the picture on Jessica's shelf had not lost much of the beauty of the sad young girl standing alone on a dirt road so many years ago. Carter wondered now if the familiarity he had attributed to her resemblance to Jessica was instead the recollection of a memory buried deep within his genes. He had so many questions.

"Not a day would go by that I didn't think of Annie in some way...some moment...wondering what she was doing, what she was thinking, if she was thinking of me. You have that now, that connection, with Jessica, and I don't want you to miss out on it."

Jack Bailey had been staring off into the distance again, as if he was watching some event unfold or seeing an old friend approach at the end of a long journey.

"I have to go soon, Carter. Autumn is a time when some things die away, never to return. For others, it is a time to rest before starting anew in the spring. I can't choose which I will be...but you can."

Carter sat there, feeling like he did when his childhood best friend told him his parents were moving away and they couldn't play together any more.

"I failed you over the years," Jack began, nodding slowly as he spoke. Jack knew this would be his last chance to converse with this grandson and did not want any questions to linger after he was gone.

"You were just as important to me as anyone else in our family, but time and life got away so quickly that you were grown and gone before we had even said 'hello.' I take responsibility for that...I owed you more...and I am so very sorry for that, Carter."

The man across from Jack Bailey fought back the emotions welling in his heart and eyes, only this time they were not the empathetic pain of another. These were his very own.

"I truly regret I will never see firsthand the man you

will become," Jack told him. "But if you don't remember, or understand, anything else from all this, I hope you keep one thing in your heart: you know me now...better than anyone in my family ever did."

Jack smiled and reached out to touch his grandson's hand one more time in this lifetime. It was at that moment that Carter Lee awakened, looking into the face of Jessica Cooper.

"Hi, there..." She murmured softly, her hand touching his. "You fell asleep. It's almost five o'clock..."

"Hi...," he murmured. "You wouldn't believe the dream I just had..."

Luckily her statement did not require a more lucid response than that. Though his mind was reeling from what he had just experienced, all he could think of at that moment was how he would love to wake up to her face for the rest of his life.

Jessica just smiled, not fully sharing the thoughts behind her eyes, but hinting at enough for Carter to know they were not unpleasant.

"Could I talk you into letting me make you dinner tonight?" he asked.

Jessica looked genuinely surprised.

"I was thinking breakfast would be nice on a cool night like tonight. I wouldn't have to pick much up at the grocery store to make you a decent meal." He smiled, brightened by the idea of another evening with her, but also to hide the confusion he was still feeling from his dream.

She feigned thinking it over, then with a quick glance to the outside hallway, kissed him quickly on the cheek.

"I would love it. I'll be ready by 6:00 if you'd like to pick me up."

Carter kissed her back, indifferent to who may see.

"I'll be there. Dress casually. Chez Bailey isn't a haute place."

With a squeeze of his hand, she turned and left the room, not looking back, but knowing his eyes remained fixed upon her.

He slowly rose up out of the chair and began pulling together his belongings. Carter would be pressed for time if he was going to make it to the grocery store and back to Jessica's by 6:00. As he slid the last of the journals and the small binder into his backpack, he realized he had been completely impervious to his grandfather, still lying peacefully in the bed beside him. Carter stared at this breathing figure for several minutes, but found he could no longer connect with the individual who lay within the bed. He now believed what made his grandfather his grandfather was gone, or was in the process of leaving, and that his body was now purposeless. At this point, it was up to nature to take its course, whenever the time was right. Carter reached over and took his grandfather's hand in the same way his grandfather had taken his in the dream. Though he would be back again, today felt like goodbye.

Carter was just pulling into Eidar's Grocery when he felt his cell phone buzzing in his right pants pocket. It took him a second to figure out what the sensation was, as the phone had been deathly quiet ever since he had left Atlanta. He quickly pulled into the first available space and, after shoving the car into 'Park,' pulled the phone from his pocket. The screen announced that he had not one, but two inbound calls, both numbers very familiar to him: one from Georgia, the other from Tennessee…his past and his present forcing their way to a decision at the very same time. He selected a line and pressed the answer key.

A light rain was beginning to fall as Carter pulled into

Jessica's driveway a few minutes after 6:00. He had found everything he wanted at the grocery, but the unexpected calls and the miscalculation of the speed of the checkout line had almost made him late. He got out of the car and was waiting with the passenger side open to help her in as she closed and locked her front door behind her.

"And they say chivalry is dead," she smiled as she took his hand and slid into the car.

When he reentered the car, she was waiting with a long kiss, this time undeterred by who may see.

"Mmmmmmmmmmmmm...I've waited all day to do that."

Carter wrapped his arms around her and held her tightly without saying a word. Jessica returned the embrace, then pulled back slightly to see his face.

"Are you OK?" she asked quietly, sensing a change in his demeanor since they were last together.

He hesitated for a moment.

"I guess so. It's been an interesting day. I'll explain in a little while." It would take awhile to explain, Carter knew, and it might take Carter even longer to come to terms with it first. But there would be time. Tonight was only about Carter and Jessica.

The menu for the evening was scrambled eggs, thick sliced bacon, biscuits, and hash browns he peeled and diced himself. In the cabinets he found an old black skillet, likely seasoned with years of his grandmother's cooking of fried chicken, cornbread, and who knew what other country staples. Carter felt at home now in the dwelling of his ancestors. That feeling was strengthened by the bond of preparing a meal that could have been served in the same kitchen many years ago.

Jessica watched him carefully divide up the eggs, browned potatoes, biscuits, and bacon equally between two plates. He sat her portion down in front of her, then returned quickly with a small plastic wine glass filled with orange juice.

"I wasn't sure which wine went with eggs, so I took the safe route." He forced a smile as she grinned at his simple humor. They dined in comfortable silence, simply enjoying their time alone. Though still in its infancy, their relationship already carried a maturity that made any obligation for small talk unnecessary. Knowing glances replaced anything that words could ever express.

"You could spoil a girl cooking like this," she teased. "Or make her fat."

What would have evoked a joking response was met with the same serious air she had sensed earlier.

"What happened today, Carter?" Jessica asked gently as she leaned toward him.

He pushed his plate back as if to clear space for the depth and breadth of his thoughts. The light sprinkling of earlier in the evening had become a steady rain, the raindrops performing a muted dance on the tin roof of the old house. Carter wondered where to begin a conversation like this. He gazed out the window before answering.

"I finished reading my grandfather's narrative today. Do you remember when I told you that what he wrote about my grandmother seemed very brief?"

She bit her lip, thinking about it.

"Yes. I think so. Why?"

"Well, I now know why I felt that way." He cleared his throat. "The love of my grandfather's life was not my grandmother…it was a girl named Annie."

Jessica unconsciously put her hand against her face in surprise.

"You're kidding. He was having an affair?"

"Oh, no. Nothing like that. He was true to my grandmother from everything I can tell."

"Then I'm confused. When did all this happen?"

Carter folded his arms and leaned against the table.

"When he was very young, apparently. They grew up together, or at least were together for many years. I think they thought they were only friends, but were really very much in love with each other. They just didn't know it. He realized it after he left for school and she thought he had left without saying goodbye on purpose. It was never the same after that...I suppose he broke her heart and she didn't forget it. He never forgot it either...or her for that matter."

She took a deep breath.

"That's so sad...is it too late? I mean, I guess it is...." she said, but the words sounded like an apology.

Carter nodded.

"Even if he weren't dying, it would be too late. She died several years ago."

"He knew this?"

"Yes. He was visiting with some old friends who grew up with them and they told him. It crushed him. She had moved out of the area years ago and never had a chance to come back."

Sadness was written across her face. Loss of a loved one was a familiar feeling to Jessica.

"Can I ask you an out-of-the-blue question, Jess?"

"Of course, Carter," she answered, a bit surprised he would even feel the need to ask.

He formed the sequence of questions carefully in his mind before continuing.

"Did you tell me your grandmother was from this area?"

"My grandmother? Yes. She grew up here, but moved to Indiana after she married my grandfather. He was working on a railroad project in the area when they met. Why?"

"Is she still living?"

Jessica looked at him curiously.

"No, she died several years ago. She had cancer."

"Non-Hodgkin's lymphoma?"

Jessica blinked.

"Yes. How in the world did you know that?"

"What was her name?"

She hesitated for a minute.

"I always called her Nana, but it was Annette. Annette Margaret Munsey. Munsey was her maiden name…"

The minute the words left her mouth, what he was trying to tell her became abundantly clear.

"You don't think…"

Anticipating her words, he answered simply.

"Yes, Jess. Your grandmother was Annie."

Neither of them said anything until Jessica broke the silence.

"Are you sure?"

"Yes, I am. How I know is the part that I don't even know how to explain. But I'll try." Carter shifted in his seat, wondering how this next phase of the conversation was going to go, but knowing it was too late to turn back.

He began telling her about waking up in his grandfather's room and seeing his grandfather standing there, about talking on the front porch of the farmhouse in a much different time, even down to the appearance of Patch and who the dog was. Carter explained how he relived his grandfather's pain and hurt, and how he recognized the girl on the road from the pictures of her grandmother. It was all out on the table now and Jessica listened with trusting patience, without a hint of disbelief.

"There was something else, Jess." He had come to the most unbelievable part of the entire story, but it was the part he wanted to believe most of all.

She waited for him to continue.

"I asked him why he did all that he did…why he wrote it all down…why he came to me."

"What did he say?" she asked quietly.

Carter took her hand.

"He told me you can gain love, you can lose love, but

you only have one chance with THE love. That everything that they had and felt is living on in us...that we can have what they wanted, but never had...and that he didn't want us to miss out on it like they did."

Hearing his words made him see that he now understood what his grandfather wanted him to grasp, and how much he felt for this woman whose hand he held.

Jessica didn't say anything for the longest time. She held his grasp as firmly as he held hers, and gently caressed his hand with her thumb. She looked at him and pulled his hand against her face.

"Do you believe it, Carter?" she asked, her eyes asking for the answer she hoped mirrored her desire.

"Yes," he said quietly, without hesitation. "I don't understand it all...but I believe it."

She pressed his hand against her face.

"I do, too."

They sat quietly together, sharing silence in the waning hours of the evening, a simple acknowledgement of what they had just shared. For the second time in as many days, however, she felt as if he was holding back. This time, however, she did not have to coax it out of him. Carter knew she deserved the truth up front.

"I have something else I need to tell you."

Carter lowered his eyes to the table.

"I had a call today. I need to go back to Atlanta tomorrow. I have some things I have to do."

A knot formed in her stomach, her heart hinting where this would lead.

"Are you coming back?" she asked, her voice failing miserably to cover any hint of the sadness that had burst upon her.

"It depends..." he answered, his voice offering no assurance either way.

She couldn't look at him now for fear he'd see the misty

tears forming in her eyes.

"On what?"

Carter got up from his chair and went over to the seat beside her. He put his arm around her chair as if to steady her, the concern on his face heightening her anxiety.

"People who live on farms really need pickup trucks instead of BMWs. So, I need to get a pickup truck. I think I'm a Ford man, so my question is…could you be with a Ford man? If a Ford just won't do, maybe we could even look at Chevy. I'm open to that…but I'm thinking Ford."

His words confused her at first, then she just stared at him.

"And dogs. Do you like dogs? I haven't had a dog in such a long time. Could you stand a dog? They can be smelly and make an incredible mess, but they do have some amazingly endearing qualities." The pace of Carter's words quickened as his excitement was revealed.

"And a farmer. I'm not even going to ask if you could see me as a farmer. It's such an outlandish proposition for a city guy, but, you know, if the Green Acres guy could do it, why can't I? Heck, he was from New York City of all places. I'm at least from the South. That should count for something, shouldn't it? Trucks, dogs, farming, and whether you can stand all that. Yes, that's it. That's what it depends on."

He smiled.

"What do you think?"

Jessica put her hands up to her face and burst forth into a bevy of sobs that rocked her body.

Carter panicked.

"Jess, what's wrong?"

Thousands of thoughts went through Carter's mind, none good. Was this too much too soon for her? Did she NOT want him around? Had he made a terrible miscalculation? Stupid, stupid, stupid, he scolded himself.

She leaned into his chest and instinctively he wrapped

his arms around her, feeling loving and protective of this woman who had captured his heart. He wondered what he had done to upset her so much.

She rested in his arms until her breathing could return to normal. Finally she looked at him.

"I thought you were telling me goodbye," she said quietly. The redness of her eyes moved him to hold her even tighter, so she would know the depth of his feelings for her.

"Oh, Jess, no. No. NO." The thought of saying goodbye to her at this point in his life, or ever, had never crossed his mind. He pressed his lips against her head and stroked her hair as he held her.

"Oh, sweetheart, no. My mother called today to tell me that a caregiver sits with my grandfather on the weekends. I didn't know that. Since my aunt will be back on Monday, she told me I didn't have to stay...if I didn't want to." He let her absorb his words.

"My boss also called, wondering when I was coming back..."

He cupped her face in his hands and gently pulled it up so she could see his eyes.

"I told him I wasn't coming back."

Jessica searched his eyes as he continued.

"I have to go back to Atlanta, but only to close out some things there. That's the only goodbye I hope I ever have to say to you," he answered simply. "No more goodbyes..."

She was quiet for several minutes, lost in his embrace, but calmer now.

"Are you sure about this? About changing your life completely and moving here?"

He smiled as he gently wiped away a stray tear that had found its way down her cheek. No words could ever convey how right this felt to him.

"I'll have enough to live on for awhile after cashing out of Associated Media...and if it gets real tight, maybe one of the local colleges will need a part-time professor. We'll figure it out." He looked like a young boy who really had no idea how he was going to do what he wanted to do, but was hell-bent on doing it. "I think where I'm going is better than where I've been. Someone very special told me that one time...I think she was right. I think I'll be OK, too. "

She touched his face and pulled him close so he could hear her.

"I love trucks, I love dogs, I love the thought of you on a tractor...and I love the feeling of falling in love with you."

On a rainy evening in the mountains of east Tennessee, a man found himself, and what mattered most to him, in the simple span of five days in autumn. Maybe no one would seek out his opinion or request his leadership on another high-dollar deal that would change the world of commerce. But none of that mattered now. She wanted him, everything that he was, and he needed her unlike anyone he had ever known. This was where he wanted to be...and where he would stay...for as long as they both shall live.

The End

Also from Aspen Mountain Publishing

For a college graduate still basking in the glow of a newly-minted diploma, the transition from campus life to full-time work can be an enlightening, if not a downright shocking, experience. You arrive at the front door of your new employer ready to contribute -- with your academic formulas, theories and practices ready to implement -- only to find a whole new education awaits you. The real world of work, and no one prepared you for this experience. Many resources help you find and get that first job out of school, but what do you do once you're IN that job? *Leaving Campus and Going to Work* provides invaluable guidance about successful behaviors and how to avoid 'derailing' your potential in that critical first year of your first job. Carefully read, considered and applied, this resource can help you not only survive your first year of full time work, but build a solid foundation of work behaviors that will benefit you your entire career.